TIGHT SQUEEZE

Frank's eyes snapped open. I must have drifted off, he realized. The clock on the wall said 1:30.

Frank was thirsty. He got out of bed and walked down the hall to the bathroom and got a drink of water. Then he stepped back out into the hall.

An arm snaked around his neck.

"Don't move," a voice whispered in his ear. "Don't speak. Don't even breathe."

The man's grip tightened, the crook of his arm pressing into Frank's neck. Two or three seconds of pressure, Frank knew, and he would pass out.

Any more than that—and he'd die.

Books in THE HARDY BOYS CASEFILES™ Series

Available from ARCHWAY Paperbacks

THE HARDY BOYS CASEFILES NO. 32

BLOOD MONEY

FRANKLIN W. DIXON

AN ARCHWAY PAPERBACK
Published by POCKET BOOKS
New York London Toronto Sydney Tokyo

AN ARCHWAY PAPERBACK *Original*

An Archway Paperback published by
POCKET BOOKS, a division of Simon & Schuster Inc.
1230 Avenue of the Americas, New York, NY 10020

ISBN: 0-671-67480-3

First Archway Paperback printing October 1989

10 9 8 7 6 5 4 3 2 1

BLOOD MONEY

Chapter

1

"WHO SAID CRIME doesn't pay?" Joe Hardy asked.

Frank Hardy turned and shot his younger brother, sitting directly behind him in the backseat, a disapproving look.

"Oh, it's not that it doesn't pay." Their father, the famous private detective Fenton Hardy, spoke up from the driver's seat. "If money is all you count, then crime certainly does pay."

"But ninety-nine percent of the time, it doesn't pay for very long," Frank added.

"I give up," Joe said, throwing his hands up in mock surrender. "All I meant was, this is a pretty elegant neighborhood for a crook to live in."

"Well, Moran didn't spend all his time

here," Fenton Hardy said, backing his car into a parking spot. "In fact, he spent the last ten years of his life in a cell about the size of your van." Looking out the back window, he glanced at Joe, who nodded sheepishly.

"I get the message, Dad."

"I knew you would," Fenton said, nosing the car up to the curb. He turned the key and slid it out. "Better lock the doors, boys. We're not in Bayport anymore."

As he stepped onto the sidewalk, Frank had to admit his brother was right about one thing. It was an expensive-looking, elegant neighborhood. Immaculate three-story townhouses, with bay windows and elaborate ironwork fences, lined both sides of the block they had parked on. The street itself was clean and quiet, with large trees (bare now that it was the middle of winter) planted at regular intervals along the sidewalk. Past the last of those trees, at the end of the block, the Manhattan skyline was clearly visible.

Since the building of these Jefferson Heights townhouses twenty years earlier, this area had become one of the most exclusive residential districts in Brooklyn. Apartment space was at a premium because the area was just over the river from Manhattan, convenient to the subways, and the neighborhood was safe.

All in all, it looked like a model for the perfectly planned urban development. But from what Fenton Hardy had been telling them on their drive from Bayport, this model of urban development had a major flaw. The beautiful townhouses had been bought by one of the country's largest criminal organizations.

"I remember when some of this block was a park," Fenton Hardy reminisced. "In the summer there were a half-dozen ball games going at one time." He was silent for a moment, then shook his head, clearing out the memories. "I don't understand this invitation. I helped to get Moran sentenced to jail twenty years ago. He delayed going for ten years, of course. But the last thing I ever expected was an invitation to Josh Moran's house."

"He can't hurt you now, Dad," Frank pointed out. "He's dead."

Which was the reason they were there. Fenton Hardy, much to his surprise, had been notified that he had been named a beneficiary in Josh Moran's will. Along with the notification had come a request to attend the reading of the will that afternoon. Frank and Joe, on break from school, had been only too eager to accompany him.

"I wonder what Moran could have left me," Fenton Hardy said.

"Probably a time bomb," Joe replied.

Frank laughed. He and Joe followed their dad across the street and up the steps of one of the few townhouses that had not been split up into apartments.

"This whole building was all Moran's," Fenton Hardy said, stepping forward and ringing the bell.

Joe whistled in admiration, just as the front door swung open and a tall, dark-haired man, dressed in a fashionable, expensive-looking suit, was revealed. He appeared to be about thirty and had the solid, trim build of an athlete.

The man smiled expectantly at Fenton. It was obvious the two didn't know each other.

Joe, on the other hand, recognized the dark-haired stranger instantly.

"I'm Fenton Hardy—these are my sons, Frank and Joe."

The man shook hands with Mr. Hardy. "Glad to meet you, sir. I'm Tommy Poletti."

Joe managed to shut his mouth, which had dropped open when the man answered the door, and mumble a quick hello.

"I'm glad you could make it today," Poletti continued, opening the door wide for them and motioning them inside. As he took their coats, Joe nudged Frank excitedly.

"Do you know who that guy is?"

Frank shook his head. "One of Moran's goons, right?"

"One of Moran's goons?" Joe shook his head excitedly, his eyes wide. "That's Tommy

4

Poletti. He was a quarterback for the University of Southern California—and won the Heisman trophy about ten years ago."

Joe was something of a fanatic about football—not surprising, considering that he played for the Bayport High football team.

"I never heard of him," Frank whispered to his brother.

"Never heard of him? He used to hold all the single-season collegiate passing records!" Joe exclaimed, a little louder than he'd intended.

"Except touchdowns in a season." Poletti turned and smiled. "But that was a long time ago."

"Joe's a running back for his high school team," Fenton Hardy put in. "A pretty good one, if I say so myself."

"Dad—" Joe protested, flushing slightly.

"Fullback, right?" Poletti asked, looking Joe up and down.

Joe nodded. "Yeah."

"We never had a good fullback at USC when I was playing," Poletti said. "Might've won a few of those Bowl games if we had." He leaned forward and spoke directly to Joe. "You want my advice, bulk up a little. They're growing linebackers bigger every year."

"I'll try," Joe said, smiling. As Poletti turned away, a sudden and obvious question occurred to Joe.

5

What was Tommy Poletti, a former Heisman trophy winner, doing mixed up with a gangster like Moran?

The question echoed in his head as Poletti led them down the hall and through a set of double doors into a large living room. About twenty people were standing there, talking to one another.

Joe recognized none of them.

This time, his father did.

"Hugh!" he called out.

A thin, dark-haired man standing by himself near the fireplace turned. When he saw Fenton Hardy, his eyes lit up.

"Fenton!"

The two men met in the middle of the room and embraced.

"Looks like your dad found an old friend," Poletti said. Just then the doorbell rang again.

"Excuse me." Poletti disappeared through the double doors.

The man their father had recognized looked somewhat older than Fenton Hardy. There were huge bags under his eyes, and as he'd crossed the room to greet Fenton Hardy, Joe noticed that he walked with a slight limp. He wore a wrinkled, ill-fitting green sport coat and baggy gray pants that hung loosely from his skeletal frame. In one hand he was carrying a drink.

Joe, with Frank a step behind, crossed the room to stand beside their father.

"It's good to see you again, Fenton," the man said, his eyes glistening a little. "These are your sons?"

Fenton Hardy nodded. "Boys, this is Hugh Nolan. He worked with me on the force."

"A long time ago. I retired more than fifteen years ago."

"Pleased to meet you, Mr. Nolan," Frank and Joe said almost simultaneously.

"You look a little like my son Ned," Nolan said to Frank, shaking hands with each of the boys. "I tried to get him to come with me today, but he just got out of the army, and . . ." He shrugged. "What's this all about, Fenton?"

"Your guess is as good as mine, Hugh."

"I don't have one," Nolan said. "To tell you the truth, I don't understand why I'm here at all—"

Nolan stopped talking abruptly, and stared over Joe's shoulder at the double doors. His face tensed.

"What's wrong, Hugh?" Fenton asked.

Joe followed the thin man's gaze.

A tall, powerfully built black man, dressed in a navy blue suit and white shirt, had just entered the room and was scanning the crowd.

"Chief Peterson!" Frank called out.

The man turned at the sound of Frank's voice and began heading toward them.

Police Chief Samuel Peterson's appearance there was no surprise to any of the Hardys. Immediately after he'd been named a beneficiary in Moran's will, Fenton Hardy had called the chief and discovered that his old partner (the two had been detectives together) had been named a beneficiary as well.

"Whatever Moran wants to leave me I guess applies to Sam as well," Fenton had said. "After all, we're the ones who put him away." The two men had talked, and both had agreed to show up for the reading.

Peterson crossed the room quickly, nodded hellos to both Frank and Joe, and shook hands warmly with their father. Fenton Hardy was clearly glad to see the chief.

Nolan, just as clearly, was not.

When the chief turned to shake hands with him, Joe felt the temperature in the room drop.

Nolan ignored Peterson's extended hand, and the chief finally lowered it and spoke.

"Hugh," he said, nodding. "It's good to see you."

"Good to see me, is it?" Nolan asked, biting off each word. "That must be it. You didn't return any of my calls fifteen years ago when I needed your help—because you were waiting to see me in person."

"I told you I had nothing to do with that decision, Hugh," Peterson said calmly.

"You could've helped me!" Nolan spat out, with such bitterness that Joe took a step aside.

What did Hugh Nolan have against Chief Peterson, anyway?

Joe glanced at his father and received a look that told him to save his questions for later.

"You've got to try to understand that was a long time ago, Hugh," Peterson was saying.

"Oh, I understand," Nolan said bitterly. "I understand, all right." He stepped closer to Peterson, till the two were only inches apart. The top of Nolan's head barely reached the collar of Peterson's jacket.

"Now you try and understand this," Hugh Nolan said.

He drew his arm back and before anyone could stop him, threw the entire contents of his drink in Chief Peterson's face!

Chapter

2

FRANK AND JOE were shocked as Nolan turned and stalked away angrily.

"Hugh—" Fenton Hardy began, then sensed it was useless to start after the man. He turned to Peterson. "Sam, are you all right?"

"Fine," Peterson said, pulling out a handkerchief and dabbing at his face. "Just fine."

"He has no right to blame you," Fenton Hardy said.

The expression in his father's eyes told Frank he'd have to save his questions for later.

He and Joe hadn't seen the chief since the events that had resulted in Fenton Hardy's kidnapping several months before, in the case *Edge of Destruction*. At that time Peterson had just entered the mayoral race in New York

City. Since then, he had withdrawn from the campaign after suffering a mild heart attack.

The chief was supposed to be taking it easy now, Frank knew, and this situation with Hugh Nolan, whatever it was, couldn't be helping matters any.

"I hate to break up the party," Fenton Hardy said. "But look who just walked in."

He nodded over his shoulder.

In the doorway at the far end of the room stood a group of five men, all in dark suits. One, clearly the leader of the group, looked as thin as Hugh Nolan, and somewhat older. But where Nolan's clothes and demeanor had indicated a man who was having trouble making ends meet, this man's bearing spoke of someone who was used to money—and knew how to enjoy it.

With him was a younger man, as powerfully built as Tommy Poletti, but with a crueler meaner face. The other three—Frank guessed they were bodyguards—formed a rough circle around them.

"The old guy is Johnny Carew. The one talking to him is his son Daniel," Peterson was saying. "They're—"

"You don't have to tell us who they are," Frank said. The Carew crime family was the most powerful on the East Coast, and Johnny was its head—a man who had supposedly controlled judges, congressmen, and even a vice-president.

At one time, Frank knew, Josh Moran had been Carew's most trusted crime lieutenant. That was before he broke away to start his own crime "family." The two groups had been feuding since then—for about twenty years. About the time that Dad got Moran convicted, Frank realized.

"Say," Joe said, nudging Frank. "Who's that?"

A pretty dark-haired woman had just entered the room from another door and was scanning the crowd.

"That's Moran's daughter, Emily." Peterson smiled. "She's a little old for you, Joe." A big heavyset man came over and spoke briefly to Emily. "Billy Delaney," the chief continued. "Moran's second-in-command. He's been running the gang the last few years, and the word is, he's not unhappy that the old man died. The big question is, now that Moran's dead, can he prevent Carew from taking back the territory Moran stole from him?"

Daniel Carew, who had been talking softly to his father, suddenly caught sight of Emily Moran. He called her name and quickly crossed the room to her side.

Carew had barely begun to talk when Emily started to move away. He grabbed her arm. An expression of anger crossed Emily Moran's face, and she coldly removed Carew's hand.

It looked as if, at least as far as she was concerned, the feud between their two families was to continue.

"If I could have your attention, ladies and gentlemen." A tall thin man, wearing wire-rimmed glasses and a bow tie, stood behind a large, antique mahogany desk at the far end of the room.

"My name is Vance Johnson, and I was Mr. Moran's lawyer. I'm here in that capacity to execute his estate—beginning with the reading of the will. If you will all take seats—"

Tommy Poletti crossed the room to sit with Emily Moran. Johnny and Daniel Carew took seats next to each other. Frank and Joe remained standing with their father and Chief Peterson. Across the room, Hugh Nolan also stood.

"Thank you for coming today." Johnson picked up a stack of papers from the desk and began reading.

" 'I, Joshua Sean Moran, being of sound mind and sound body, do hereby bequeath the entire body of my estate, its assets and capital, to my only daughter, Emily—' "

"No surprises there," Daniel Carew interjected. Tommy Poletti shot him a dirty look.

" 'With this exception. I have set aside in a safe-deposit box ten million dollars in cash.

This money is to be divided equally among the following individuals: Hugh Nolan, Johnny Carew, Daniel Carew, Samuel Peterson, Fenton Hardy, Thomas Poletti, and William Delaney.' ''

There was a moment of stunned silence. Frank and his father exchanged a puzzled glance. Johnson continued reading.

'' 'These shares will be payable three months from the date of the reading of this will. They may not be transferred or assigned, nor may they be renounced, except in the single following instance.' ''

Johnson looked up over his glasses. '' 'The only way one of the named beneficiaries shall not receive his due share of this money is if he meets his demise before the aforementioned date. In that event, the shares of the remaining beneficiaries will increase proportionately.' ''

Fenton Hardy didn't look pleased—nor did any of the other people named as beneficiaries.

"Say it again—in English, Van," Daniel Carew said.

"It's simple enough," Tommy Poletti interjected. "Everyone whose name was called is due a share of ten million dollars—if he can stay alive for the next three months."

"This is why Moran wanted you all here," Frank said, his eyes wide. "Revenge."

Fenton Hardy nodded grimly. "He's made it open season on every one of us."

Chapter

3

JOE STUDIED THE COLLECTION of gangsters assembled in the room. It wasn't hard to figure what the next three months would be like.

With ten million dollars at stake, murder would be in the air.

Chief Peterson rose, his face twisted in anger. "I don't know about anyone else, but I don't want any part of this will—or that ten million dollars."

"I don't intend to become involved either," Fenton Hardy said.

"We should all refuse to take part in Moran's sick little exercise," the chief added.

At that precise moment, Joe turned and saw Hugh Nolan's face. Clearly, he wanted his slice of Moran's fortune.

"If you're so uncomfortable with your

share, you could give it to me, Chief," Daniel Carew offered. "In three months, of course."

"I'd rather burn it," Peterson said.

"That's against the law," Daniel said, smiling wickedly. "I'd have to report you. Besides—if some screwball wants to leave me a share of ten million dollars, who am I to argue?" He smiled at Emily. "No offense."

"Watch your language, Carew," Poletti said. "How about a little respect for the dead?"

"You're a fine one to talk about respect for the dead," Carew replied. His eyes went to Emily. "Why don't you give the lady a decent amount of time to mourn her father before you marry her—"

"You need to learn some manners, pal," Poletti said, springing to his feet.

"From you?" Carew asked. "Don't make me laugh."

Emily put a hand on Poletti's arm. He shrugged it off, and stood waiting, his eyes blazing.

Joe wondered if the former Heisman winner knew how dangerous it was for him to be threatening the son of one of organized crime's biggest kingpins.

"Tommy, Mr. Carew, please—" Johnson began.

"Daniel!" Johnny Carew, who had remained virtually silent during the reading of the will and the exchanges that followed, now spoke up for the first time. "Apologize to Mr. Poletti—and to Miss Moran."

The elder Carew's voice was clipped and couldn't hide the fact that Carew was furious with his son. Daniel mumbled a reluctant apology, first to Poletti, who accepted reluctantly, and then Emily.

The two men sat down again.

"I, for one, intend to honor Joshua's wishes regarding the disposition of his estate," Johnny Carew continued. "If he wanted all of us"—he raised a hand and held it out palm up—"to share equally in his wealth, that is how we will share it."

"You can't be serious," Peterson said. "You know Moran wants us to kill each other for that money—"

"I am perfectly willing to accept my share of Josh's estate," Carew continued, ignoring the chief. "I hope everyone else here will do the same."

"None of us wants any trouble, Chief," Delaney added. "But I'm not giving up my share, either."

Peterson shook his head in disgust.

"I'm afraid the whole question is beside the point. It's quite impossible for any of you to renounce your shares." Johnson placed the papers he'd been reading from into a manila folder on the desk. "Mr. Moran has written his will so that it will be impossible for any of you to step aside as a beneficiary. The shares of the other beneficiaries only increase if—"

"If we die," Daniel Carew said.

"Yes, that's essentially correct." Johnson cleared his throat. "If there are no other questions . . ."

Joe shook his head. Why had Moran made Poletti a target? For that matter, why was Delaney, Moran's right-hand man, a beneficiary as well? He doubted that Johnson had the answers to those questions.

The lawyer cleared his throat again and looked around the room. "I thank you all for coming. We'll meet back here in three months—at which time we'll discuss the formal distribution of Mr. Moran's estate."

The gathering broke up quickly after that. The Hardys, after seeing Chief Peterson off, found themselves outside on the street just as Hugh Nolan emerged from the brownstone.

"Don't say it, Fenton," Nolan said as he reached the bottom of the steps. His limp was much more pronounced now, and he was clearly straining with each step.

"You know I've got to, Hugh," Fenton Hardy said. He stepped forward to give Nolan a hand, but the older man waved him off. "Sam did everything he legally could to see that you got your money. He got outvoted—"

"I don't want to hear it!" Nolan snarled. He bit his lip then and was silent a moment. When he spoke again, he was much calmer. "Sorry, Fenton. I shouldn't have snapped at you—or thrown the drink at Sam. Just lost my temper again." He checked his watch. "Anyway, I've got to go."

"It was good to see you, Hugh." Fenton took Nolan's hand and shook it vigorously.

"And you, too, Fenton. But I'm afraid I've made a bad impression on your sons," he said, turning to Frank and Joe. "Maybe I can make it up to you next time by telling you some stories of when your father was a rookie cop."

"Next time?" Joe asked.

"Why—three months from now."

And with that, Nolan turned and walked off down the street.

"Looks like he's anxious to get his share of Moran's cash, Dad," Joe said as they climbed into the backseat of their gray four-door sedan.

"I'm afraid things haven't gone well for Hugh for the past twenty years since he was charged with taking bribes," Fenton replied. "His wife left him, there were problems over his pension, and he had to retire early without getting it."

"So I gathered," Frank said. "And he blames Chief Peterson for those problems."

"That's right." His father checked the rearview mirror and pulled out into traffic. "I wouldn't doubt Hugh Nolan could put his share of that money to good use."

"Who couldn't?" Joe asked. "Seven people, ten million dollars, that's—"

"Almost a million and a half each," Frank said.

"I for one don't intend to share in any of that money," Fenton Hardy said firmly. "As soon as we get home, I'm going to put in a call to my lawyer and see what we can do."

"Johnson said you couldn't change the terms," Frank pointed out.

"Then I'll give the money to charity," Fenton Hardy said. "And that will be the end of it."

Joe, in the backseat, watched out the rear window as the skyline of Manhattan disappeared. He thought about the group of people they'd seen that day and the amount of money at stake.

Somehow, he knew his father was wrong. That wouldn't be an end to it.

A month and a half passed.

It was a blustery morning, two days into winter break, and Frank and Joe had come to New York City to do some research at the public library. They were browsing through a subway newsstand, waiting for a subway train: Frank bought a computer magazine; Joe, one of the New York City papers. They had just sat down in the subway when Joe tossed the paper he was reading onto Frank's lap, right on top of his magazine.

"Take a look at this," Joe said.

"Crime Kingpin Murdered," the headline screamed. Beneath it, in bold print, the article continued.

Daniel Carew, reputed heir to the crime family run by his father, Johnny Carew, was gunned down late yesterday evening in front of his Brooklyn home.

Frank looked up.

"Read on," his brother said. "There's a lot more."

Frank picked up the paper.

The police discovered Carew's body on the stoop of his Brooklyn brownstone. He had been shot once in the chest. The police are holding Tommy Poletti, former Heisman trophy winner, who, according to police reports, had argued violently with Daniel Carew earlier that day.

Frank shook his head. "Tommy Poletti—a killer?"

"I don't believe it either," Joe said.

Frank continued reading and learned that the police had found no gun. However, Carew's own revolver, which "he always carried with him," according to sources, was missing.

The paper suggested that the shooting might be the start of a gang war over Joshua Moran's territory, now that he was dead.

But Frank knew there was another, better motive for Carew's murder.

It seemed that the game of killer-take-all that his father had predicted was beginning.

"I bet Chief Peterson has involved himself in this case," Frank said.

"And I bet you're right." Joe nodded. "Which makes me think we ought to take a little detour."

Frank nodded. "They're holding Poletti at the eighty-fourth precinct house in Brooklyn," he said. "And I bet that's where we find Peterson."

They got off at the next stop to change trains and an hour later were standing in front of the precinct house on Gold Street.

"This is the place," Joe said. "Now, how do we get in to see Chief Peterson?"

"I'll think of something," Frank said, just as a limousine was pulling up next to them. Emily Moran emerged.

"Miss Moran," Frank called out.

She turned and stared at Frank and Joe, a puzzled expression on her face.

"I'm Frank Hardy, and this is my brother

Joe—we were at the reading of your father's will. . . ."

"Of course," Emily said distractedly. She looked exhausted: dark circles formed half-moons below her eyes, and her skin was sallow, as if she hadn't slept all night. "You'll have to forgive me— This whole business with Tommy—that the police think he's involved in murder . . ." She shook her head.

Frank smiled understandingly. "It seems a little unlikely to us, as well."

Someone cleared his throat behind the three-some. "And who are the two of you?"

A thin man with a close-cropped black beard, who must have just emerged from the precinct house, was standing on the steps, eyeing the Hardys suspiciously.

Frank approached him, leaving Emily standing next to the car with Joe.

"I'm Frank Hardy," he said, extending his hand.

"Detective Mike Lewis," the man said, shaking Frank's hand firmly. He looked at Frank closely, then snapped his fingers. "You're Fenton Hardy's kid, aren't you?"

Frank nodded, somewhat surprised. "How did you—"

"You look just like him," Lewis said. The detective nodded in Emily Moran's direction and lowered his voice. "I can guess what brings you here."

"You'd probably guess right," Frank said. "We want to know if this shooting ties in to Josh Moran's will."

Lewis hesitated. "You know, I really can't talk about the case with you. . . ." His voice trailed off.

"I understand," Frank said. "But if Chief Peterson okays it?"

Lewis smiled. "Anything's okay then. He's just inside. If he doesn't have a problem talking about the case with you there, then I—"

"Good," Frank said. "Lead the way."

The four of them entered the precinct house together.

"First I've got to pick up Poletti," Lewis said. He pointed to his right. "The holding cells are this way. Miss Moran?" She nodded that she wanted to accompany the detective.

"Actually, I'd like to talk to the chief first," Frank said. He wanted to find out just how strong the case was against Tommy Poletti— information he didn't think he'd get with both Poletti and Emily Moran present. Joe indicated he'd go with Lewis and Emily.

"The chief's in the office at the top of the stairs—follow this corridor—you can't miss it."

To Joe, the precinct house looked like his high school. The cinder-block halls were painted the same dull beige and decorated (more accurately, not decorated) in the same dull style.

Off to the right was a sign that said Holding Cells, with an arrow pointing down the stairs. Lewis, who had obviously been to the station many times before, led them down a flight of stairs and then into a long, narrow basement corridor. They were about halfway down it when Joe stopped short.

"Did you hear something?" he asked.

Lewis and Emily Moran looked at each other and shook their heads. "I didn't," Lewis said.

"Wait." Joe held up his hand. "There it is again." He listened closely for a second, then turned back the way they'd come and stopped in front of a door marked Utility Closet.

Faint thumping noises could be heard coming from inside.

Joe tried the knob. It wouldn't budge.

"Hey!" He banged loudly on the door, then threw his weight against it.

In response, there came a renewed series of thumps, louder and more insistent than before.

"In here!" Joe said excitedly. "There's somebody trapped inside!"

Chapter

4

"I DON'T BELIEVE IT," Chief Peterson said. He was sitting behind a large gray metal desk, a lot of papers fanned out in front of him that he had obviously been studying until Frank interrupted him. Now he was staring up at the source of the interruption with a half-shocked, half-pleased expression on his face.

Frank Hardy stood in the doorway of the chief's borrowed office, looking slightly ill at ease.

"This case isn't twelve hours old, and the boy genius is here to help already." Chief Peterson gathered up some of the papers he'd been studying and slipped them into a manila folder. "Where's your brother? Working with the detectives?" the chief asked, smiling to let Frank know he was kidding.

Frank smiled back and nodded. "He is. He's downstairs with Lewis and Emily Moran."

"I give up!" Peterson threw up his hands. "What took you so long?"

"We just got into town."

"Well, you might as well have a seat," the chief said. He indicated a chair in front of the desk.

"Do you mind if I ask you a few questions about the shooting?"

Peterson laughed out loud and shook his head. "Matter of fact, I was just going to call your dad and tell him about this."

"So you also think this has something to do with Moran's will?" Frank leaned forward, catching a glimpse of the police report on the shooting, which lay open on the desk. Poletti's record was the top sheet of the file.

"No, I think this has nothing to do with the will," Peterson replied.

"But I thought you said—"

"I was going to tell your dad not to worry when he read about this. As far as we can tell, this is a case of jealousy. Two men fighting over the same girl."

"The papers thought that it might be the start of a gang war," Frank said.

Peterson pursed his lips. "I don't think so. Poletti's only involvement with the Moran crime family seems to be with Emily."

Frank nodded. "The papers also said you hadn't charged him with anything yet."

"That's true," the chief said. "But Lewis and I are hoping he'll confess—the evidence is pretty convincing."

"I don't know," Frank said slowly. "I just can't see Poletti killing Carew—"

"Why? Because he's a former Heisman winner? A lot of things could have happened to him since then. We don't really know anything about him," Peterson said.

Frank nodded a little sheepishly.

Just then, a bell began ringing outside in the hall. Frank raised his eyebrows. "What's that?" he asked.

"That," Peterson said, standing up, "is the coffee cart—more popularly known around here as the 'roach coach.' " He smiled at Frank. "Come on—I'll buy you a soda."

Frank rose and followed him, but he wasn't sure he wanted to eat anything from a "roach coach."

"How could anyone get locked inside a closet—inside a police station?" Emily asked.

"I don't know if it is a 'someone,' " Lewis said, shaking his head. He rapped the door sharply with his knuckles, then stood for a moment with his ear pressed to the door, listening. "But something's in there, all right. I'll see if I can find some keys." He disappeared down the hall.

"Hang on!" Joe yelled at the door. "We'll have you out of there in a second!"

In fact, it took more than five minutes for Lewis to return. All the time Joe and Emily Moran stood, listening to the muffled thumping on the other side of the locked door.

Finally Lewis arrived with a ring of keys about the size of a softball; the fifth key opened the door.

A man, hands and feet bound behind his back and a gag stuffed into his mouth, lay on his stomach next to the door.

Lewis rolled him over.

"It's Ed!" Lewis said, bending down and undoing the man's gag. Joe helped Lewis untie the man's bonds and get him into a sitting position. The man began taking in huge gulps of air.

"Take it easy," Lewis said, kneeling down by him. "Are you all right?"

"What happened?" Joe asked.

"Beats me," Ed said, his words punctuated by faint gasps. "I was coming out of the service elevator when I hear this noise behind me. Next thing I know, I'm lying in this closet all tied up—with a whopper of a headache. Somebody thumped me over the head but good!"

Lewis looked puzzled. "What would anyone

want to knock you out for?'' he asked, shaking his head.

"What do you do around here?'' Joe asked, kneeling down next to Ed.

"Him?'' Lewis spoke first, before Ed could answer. "He's from the food service company. Runs the coffee cart.''

"What can I get you today?''

The coffee cart, Frank saw, was similar to the pushcarts that were rolled up and down the aisles of airplanes. This one had sandwiches and an assortment of beverages and snacks.

"Where's Ed?'' Chief Peterson asked.

"Oh—he called in sick today,'' the man pushing the cart said. He was a couple of inches shorter and a few years older than Chief Peterson, with graying hair that hung almost to his shoulders. He had on a white button-down shirt and black pants.

"Anything serious?'' Peterson asked, rummaging through the contents of the cart. He picked up a sugared doughnut and looked at it longingly.

"Might be—I wouldn't count on seeing him for a while,'' the man said, shrugging. "That's fresh,'' he said, pointing at the doughnut the chief had picked up.

"Looks it,'' Peterson said. "But I'm on a diet.'' He patted his stomach and put down the doughnut. "Give me a decaffeinated coffee—

black. And I'll take one of these." He picked up a small bran muffin and shook his head ruefully. "Good for the old ticker, they tell me," he said.

The man behind the cart nodded and handed Peterson his coffee. "That's what I hear, too. You got heart problems?"

Peterson shrugged. "Nothing serious."

"Good. Just make sure you take it easy," the man behind the cart said.

"I plan to," Peterson said. He raised the cup to his lips and took a sip. "That's good coffee. Almost tastes like the real thing."

"I'm glad you like it," the man behind the cart said. "It's a fresh pot." His eyes were the most piercing shade of blue—almost a purple, really—that Frank had ever seen. They were also remarkably unlined for a man who otherwise looked to be in his late forties.

"You want something?" the chief asked Frank.

"A cup of coffee, maybe?" the man asked.

Frank shook his head. "Joe and I had a big lunch."

"Okay, then." The chief nodded to the man behind the cart. "See you later."

"Take it easy," the man said, and disappeared down the hall.

Frank and Peterson returned to the office the chief was using and sat down again.

Peterson took a bite of the muffin, and then

another sip of his coffee. "Anyway, no, I don't think this has anything to do with the will. We have about fifteen witnesses who saw Carew and Poletti get into a shoving match on the Brooklyn Heights promenade early yesterday evening. Poletti threatened Carew in front of all of them."

Frank nodded. "One of the other beneficiaries could be setting Poletti up—"

"In order for somebody to get a lot more money, he'd have to knock off Johnny Carew and Billy Delaney—the heads of two of the largest East Coast crime families. Nobody's that dumb." Peterson wiped a hand across his forehead and grimaced. "It feels hot in here all of a sudden. Did they turn up the heat?"

Frank shook his head. "Feels the same to me."

The chief loosened his tie and unbuttoned the collar of his shirt. "Anyway, not only would they have to kill Carew and Delaney, they'd have to get at yours truly, the chief of police. And how are they going to do that?"

"I see your point, but—"

Frank looked at Peterson. The chief was really sweating now, and he also looked very gray. "Are you all right?"

Peterson shook his head. "I'm not sure. I feel dizzy, I—" He stood suddenly and gasped, swaying on his feet.

Frank was at his side in an instant to help

ease him back down in his chair. The back of Peterson's shirt was drenched in sweat.

"Frank," the chief said slowly, a look of horror spreading across his face. "I'm having a heart attack!"

Chapter

5

"I JUST HOPE whoever's got the cart hasn't wrecked it," Ed said, leading Lewis down a long, narrow hallway. Joe trailed a few paces behind; they had left Emily with one of the officers in charge of the holding cells. "I'm responsible for whatever happens to it, you know."

"Let's just find the guy," Lewis said. "Then we'll worry about what he's done."

And why, Joe added silently.

The basement of the police station was a maze of identical cinder-block corridors. Again, Joe was reminded of high school: any second, he expected to hear bells ring and to see students pour out of classes into the halls. There were even lockers along one wall, he saw.

As they crossed another corridor, Joe heard a noise off to his left. He turned and looked in that direction.

About fifty feet away a man in a white shirt had his back to them. He had long gray hair and was stooped over, and he was pushing a food cart with a coffee pot on top. A police officer was walking next to him, and the two were talking animatedly.

"Hey," Ed said, stopping so suddenly Joe almost crashed into him. "That's my cart!"

"Hey!" Joe yelled. The man in the white shirt and the police officer both turned.

"Stop that man!" Lewis called out.

The officer recognized Lewis. With a puzzled look on his face, he reached for the man walking beside him, putting a hand on his shoulder to detain him.

The man in the white shirt straightened up, and it was as if he'd shed twenty years. He moved like lightning, spinning to free himself from the policeman's grasp. He continued his spin into a side-kick. His foot slammed into the officer's chest, sending him crashing against the wall.

The officer slumped to the ground and lay still.

The man in the white shirt shoved the cart out of his path and raced off down the hallway. The cart smashed into the wall, spilling plastic-wrapped pastries and coffee all over.

"Hey!" Ed yelled. "Look what that guy did!"

"Forget it—go get help," Lewis told Ed, physically turning him around and pointing him in the direction they'd come from.

The second the officer hit the wall, Joe was racing full tilt after his assailant.

As he sped through corridors, Joe quickly realized two things. The man he was chasing was fast—and he couldn't be as old as his stooped-over posture had suggested. Or if he was old, he was in fantastic shape, because Joe, who was anything but slow, was losing ground.

He bore down harder. The corridors were deserted. As Joe ran, the only sounds he was aware of were his own labored breathing and the squeaking of his sneakers on the linoleum floor.

He was still losing ground, though he told himself that all he had to do was keep the man in sight—after all, he was trapped in a police station. How could he possibly escape? Up ahead, Joe saw his quarry disappear to the left, as the corridor they were running down ended.

Joe slowed. Lewis jogged up beside him, breathing heavily.

"He turned down here," Joe said as they came to the end of the corridor.

Off to their left, about twenty feet away, was a bank of elevators—and the mysterious man in the white shirt, who stood there, waiting silently.

"You can't get away," Lewis called out. "Why don't you make it easy on yourself?"

The man said nothing. He seemed completely unconcerned by their presence—as if they couldn't do a thing to stop him, whatever he decided to do.

"Give it up," Joe added, continuing to move toward him. Behind them, he could hear running footsteps—more police, no doubt, coming to help them. "You're outnumbered."

The ghost of a smile crossed the man's lips—and at that second the elevator doors opened.

The man stepped inside quickly.

Joe, who was about five feet away, sprang toward him, just as the door was starting to slide shut.

The man spun into another side-kick. But Joe was ready for it. He sidled out of the way, so the kick only caught him a glancing blow.

It still felt as if he'd been struck with a lead weight. He bounced off the closing elevator door and landed on the floor just outside the car.

Joe struggled to his feet and launched himself into the elevator. Something hard slammed into his stomach, knocking the wind from him. He reached up, trying to grab the man to stop him from getting away. He did manage to clasp something—just as another kick sent him spinning backward through the open elevator door.

Whatever he'd grabbed came with him.

Joe landed on the ground, flat on his back. He looked at what he was holding in his hand, then up at Lewis.

"It's a wig," Joe said, holding up a clump of gray hair. "The guy was wearing a wig."

"Stay calm, Chief," Frank said.

"My pills, Frank," Peterson gasped. He was having trouble catching his breath now. "Nitroglycerin—my coat pocket." He reached up with his right arm and shakily pointed to the back of the door.

Frank unhooked the coat and reached into the pocket to pull out a small bottle.

"That's it," the chief said. "Give them to me—quick." He took the bottle from Frank and tried to pop the cap off. But his arm was shaking so badly now that he dropped it on the floor.

"Hurry!"

Frank picked up the bottle and got a pill out. He placed it beneath the chief's tongue.

"It's not working," Peterson said, and now there was panic in his voice.

From his CPR course, Frank knew that whatever panic the chief was feeling was only making his condition worse.

"Try to stay calm," Frank said. "I'll get

help." A group of three officers was standing just outside the door. "Call an ambulance!" he yelled. "The chief's having a heart attack!"

They stared at him for a second, trying to place him.

But before Frank knew it, they were inside the office, snapping out orders. Two pulled the chief to his feet; the third spoke to Frank.

"We'll take a squad car."

The two officers carrying Chief Peterson held him as easily as if he were a baby and practically ran through the station and outside with him.

Would they get to the hospital in time to save him? Frank wondered as he climbed into a squad car. They were following the one carrying the chief. His mind ran on that treadmill until they arrived at the hospital emergency room. He and the police officers he'd ridden with spent half an hour in the waiting room, not knowing anything.

Finally one of the emergency room technicians emerged.

"He's over the worst of it," the man told them. "We seem to have stabilized his heartbeat. Took a long time to do it, though," he said, shaking his head. "Anyway, if you hadn't gotten him here so quickly—"

Someone tapped Frank on the shoulder just then.

Joe was standing there, looking concerned.

"Heard all about it at the station," he said. "How's the chief?"

"He's going to make it." Frank studied his brother, who looked somewhat disheveled. "What happened? Did you run all the way?"

"We had a little excitement of our own," Joe said. He told him about the intruder at the police station. "Anyway, by the time we got out to the street, the guy was gone. And nobody had seen him or anything." Joe shook his head. "Lewis is still trying to figure out why this guy was so anxious to impersonate a coffee vendor. . . ." His voice trailed off suddenly as he caught the look in his brother's eye.

In Frank's mind, things were starting to click into place. "The chief started having his attack a few minutes after drinking his coffee," he said.

"You think he might have been poisoned?" Joe asked.

"All we can do is find out."

They waited until Peterson's own doctor had arrived and finished briefing the police. Then they pulled her aside and told her about their suspicions.

"Chief Peterson's been very good about taking care of himself," she said thoughtfully. "I'm surprised that this attack came on so suddenly. Let me run a blood test, check for poison. It'll take a couple of hours," she added. "So make yourselves comfortable."

By this time a large crowd of police officers and relatives had assembled outside the emergency room. Among them, Frank caught sight of Detective Lewis and Chief Peterson's wife, Anne. He and Joe crossed to her side and sat down with her, to wait for the test results. Almost two hours to the minute, they had their answer.

"The chief was definitely poisoned," his doctor said. "We found traces of an amphetamine in his system. The drug would have simulated all the symptoms of a heart attack— palpitations, shortness of breath, chest pain, and would probably have been fatal to him, without his nitroglycerin pills and prompt treatment. If you hadn't gotten him here so quickly . . ." Her voice trailed off.

Frank thought of the unexpected circumstances that had led him to Brooklyn and to his talk with the chief and what might have happened if he hadn't been there to reach those nitro pills when the chief started having his attack.

"You think this might have something to do with the will?" Joe asked, pulling his brother aside.

Frank pursed his lips. "I do. Granted, there are probably a lot of people who'd like to see the chief dead, but this, right on the heels of Carew getting shot—"

Joe broke in. "I think we'd better call Dad to make sure he's okay."

Frank nodded grimly. "And then we'd better find out a lot more about that man in the white shirt—before he strikes again."

Chapter
6

FRANK SPENT the next forty-five minutes on the phone to Bayport.

The first fifteen minutes he spent reassuring his aunt Gertrude that he and Joe were fine. Then he spent fifteen minutes reassuring his mother that their schoolwork wasn't suffering. Finally he was able to speak to his father and reassure himself that Fenton Hardy was all right. Frank briefed his father on the mysterious goings-on at the police station that afternoon. When Fenton heard Chief Peterson was in the hospital, he decided to drive down to see him. By nine o'clock all three Hardys were assembled in Peterson's hospital room.

"I got here as quickly as I could," Fenton Hardy said. He laid a hand on Samuel Peterson's shoulder. "And I'll have you know I had to miss one of Laura's foreign film festivals to get here.''

Peterson laughed. "It's good to see you." The chief still looked a little weak, but he was in good spirits. "And I'm flattered you came just to make sure I was all right."

"I didn't," Fenton said. "I came to see Anne, too." Peterson's wife was sitting in a chair on the other side of the bed, holding her husband's hand. Frank thought she looked a little worse than the chief at that point. "And my boys, of course."

"If it wasn't for that one boy of yours," Peterson said, nodding toward Frank, "I might not be here now."

Frank flushed beet red.

"And if it wasn't for the other"—Peterson nodded at Joe now—"we wouldn't have found out that I was poisoned."

Now it was Joe's turn to blush.

"They'll make good detectives someday," Fenton said. His expression turned serious then. "There's actually another reason I rushed in," he said. "After hearing about Daniel Carew, and now this—"

"I know," Peterson said, looking at Frank. "I may have been wrong. The Carew killing might have something to do with Moran's will."

"So Poletti has to be innocent," Joe said,

thinking fast. "He couldn't have drugged you."

"Maybe. He could have hired someone to poison me," the chief pointed out.

"Or there could be more than one killer among the beneficiaries. More than one person willing to commit murder to increase his share," Fenton put in.

"That's a scary idea," Peterson said. His brow creased as he thought. "First thing tomorrow, I'll see about getting some kind of report together on where all those beneficiaries are—"

"You'll do nothing of the sort!" Anne Peterson said. She looked angry. "Sam Peterson, you're supposed to be taking it easy!"

"You're right, dear. I'll have someone else take care of it." He and Fenton exchanged a hurried glance, and Fenton nodded, indicating he'd pick up the slack.

"You be careful, Fenton. It couldn't hurt to take precautions—"

"I will," Mr. Hardy said. "And I'll call Hugh Nolan, if you like," he offered.

"Good," Peterson said. "Any warning from me and he'd be likely to disregard on principle."

"All right," Fenton said. "We'll get started right away. Good night, Sam. Good night, Anne."

When they got out into the hall, Fenton

spoke privately to his sons. He'd rushed right in to see the chief as soon as he'd gotten to the hospital and hadn't had a chance to talk to them yet.

"I'm very proud of both of you" was the first thing he said. "Now, what can you tell me about this man who poisoned the chief?"

"Not much, I'm afraid," Frank said. "He was pretty well disguised."

"Yeah," Joe said. "First time I saw the guy, I thought he was about fifty. But he moved like a young guy. Whoever he was, he was really well trained in karate—or something."

"Something?" Frank asked.

"You know—kung fu, tae kwon do—one of those martial arts. I knew what he was going to do, but I couldn't stop him. It was like I was moving in slow motion the whole time."

Fenton turned to his eldest son. "Frank? Anything else?"

"Not really. Just like Joe, I thought he was a lot older at first, but then—" He shook his head. "I don't know. He could have been twenty-five or fifty-five, I really couldn't tell."

"You said he had blue eyes," Joe offered.

"That's right—I noticed them right away," Frank said. "They were so—" He looked up at his dad. "They were too blue," he said suddenly. "I think we were supposed to notice them."

Fenton nodded. "Probably tinted contact lenses. Sounds like a pro."

"What do we do now?" Frank asked.

"*We* don't do anything," Fenton said. "I'm going to make sure Hugh Nolan's all right—and then do a little detecting on the case. And you two are getting on the last train back to Bayport."

"We did come into the city to use the library," Frank pointed out. "And it's a little late to do that now."

Joe smiled. "Looks like you're stuck with us—at least until tomorrow."

Fenton nodded. "All right," he said. "Let's find a hotel. But first, I want to call Hugh Nolan. There's a phone down the hall."

"Dad, wait," Frank said.

Fenton faced his eldest son.

"What happened between Nolan and Peterson that Nolan hates him so much?" Frank asked hesitantly.

"*Hate* isn't the word I'd use." Fenton shook his head ruefully. "It goes back twenty years—to that case Sam and I had, the one that eventually put Moran away."

"You've never told us anything about it," Frank said.

"For good reason," Fenton replied. "It was a particularly ugly case—one I don't like to think about too much. A fire happened in what used to be one of the worst sections of Brooklyn. Where the Jefferson Heights townhouses are now."

"That neighborhood where Moran lives?" Joe asked incredulously. "That was a bad section of town?"

"It sure was," his father replied. "But the townhouses were planned to change all that. They were supposed to revitalize the whole neighborhood. But there was one small problem—there were already apartments there, with families living in them." He sighed deeply. "It was a mess. The developers were fighting to have the apartments condemned, the families living in them were fighting to stay. All the papers followed it for months. For a while it looked as if the whole deal might fall through.

"Then one night, there was a fire. Half a block of those tenements burned to the ground. Twelve people died. And the Jefferson Heights townhouses got built after all."

"How did you get involved?"

"Sam and I were assigned to the case about two days after the fire, when evidence of arson was discovered. We found out immediately that a lot of the families had been complaining about harassment by the developers for weeks, but nothing had been done. Hugh Nolan was the officer in charge of investigating the original harassment charges.

"I went to Hugh—we'd known each other

for some time—and he assured me there was no harassment. Sam felt differently. He thought the developers had paid off Hugh to look the other way. He said as much.''

''And you? What did you think?''

''Well—there were a lot of suspicious incidents, but I'm from the old school. Innocent until proven guilty. And we never found anything linking Hugh with the developers. Then later, Hugh came forward with evidence that helped us prove Josh Moran had ordered those fires, and even Sam had to admit he'd been wrong to accuse Hugh. But it was too late to salvage Hugh's career—the damage had been done.''

Joe frowned. ''Was that when Moran still worked for Carew?''

Fenton nodded. ''That's right. The townhouses were Carew's project—from start to finish. He bankrolled the developers, and we know he had to have ordered Moran to set the fires. Of course, we could never prove any connection there. With all the legal delays and stalling tactics, it took ten years for Moran's case to come to trial. But he did end up behind bars. As for Hugh . . .'' Fenton sighed. ''He took early retirement and missed out on his pension. He wanted Sam to intercede on his behalf, but . . .''

Frank nodded silently.

''Anyway,'' Fenton said, checking his

watch, "I'd better make that call before it gets too late."

Hugh Nolan was fine and happy to hear from Fenton. When he heard they were in town, he insisted on putting them up for the night in his small Lower East Side apartment.

"It's not much," he said, smiling as he led the Hardys into the living room after giving them a brief tour. They all took seats. "But it's home."

"It's a lot better than staying at a hotel," Fenton said. "Thanks."

"You're quite welcome. Now—you never did tell me why you were in town."

Fenton leaned forward in his chair. "Hugh— have you heard about Daniel Carew?"

Nolan grunted his assent. "Sure. Someone should have plugged him ten years ago, if you ask me."

"Be that as it may," Fenton said. He took a deep breath. "There was another incident today. Someone tried to poison Sam Peterson."

"What!"

"Frank and Joe were with him when it happened. That's why I'm here—they called me."

Nolan's face had gone pale. "Sam was poisoned? Is he all right?"

Fenton nodded. "He'll be fine. We just left him." He took a deep breath. "Hugh, we think both incidents might be connected."

"Moran's will, you mean."

"Exactly. Our murderer may be someone who wants to increase his share of that money very badly."

Nolan was silent for a moment. "I won't kid you, Fenton. I could really use my share of that money. But anyone who'd do something like this . . ."

Fenton nodded. "We all—all the beneficiaries—have to be especially careful. It might not be a bad idea for you to get out of town for a while."

"I guess you're right—though I'm not sure where I'd go—"

"Well," Fenton said, "I think we ought to talk to the police about that. If you like, I'll speak to them tomorrow."

Frank saw Nolan's face tighten involuntarily. Then he relaxed.

"All right," he said. "I'll leave the details to you." He stood and stretched. "I'm going to turn in now. You three can stay up if you want—"

"No, we'll turn in, too," Fenton said. He looked pointedly at Joe and Frank. "The boys have to get an early start tomorrow—they have work to do at the library."

Frank checked the clock on the wall. It was after eleven, so he decided not to argue with his father—in spite of his desire to talk about the case some more.

They all said good night. Fenton Hardy and Joe each took a twin bed in the smaller bedroom, while Frank settled in on the living room couch.

But he wasn't ready to sleep just yet. He wanted to sort through the day's events before going to bed. That story his father had told— about the arson in which twelve people were killed, and Moran's will—he'd bet the two incidents were somehow connected.

Frank yawned. Suddenly he was having trouble staying awake.

He thought about Hugh Nolan. For someone who supposedly hated Chief Peterson, he sure looked concerned when we told him that the chief had been poisoned. . . .

Frank's eyes snapped open. I must have drifted off, he realized. The clock on the wall said 1:30.

He was thirsty. He got out of bed and walked down the hall to the bathroom to get a drink of water. Then he stepped back out into the hall.

An arm snaked around his neck.

"Don't move," a voice whispered in his ear. "Don't speak. Don't even breathe."

The man's grip tightened, the crook of his arm pressing into Frank's neck. Two or three seconds of pressure, Frank knew, and he would pass out.

Any more than that—and he'd die.

Chapter

7

FRANK'S FIRST THOUGHTS were that he'd stumbled into the person who'd been killing the beneficiaries and that he was about to become the killer's next victim.

"Who are you, and what are you doing here?" The man's viselike grip tightened slightly, prompting Frank to answer.

"My name is Frank Hardy—I'm a guest here," he choked out.

"Hardy?" Frank heard the question in the man's voice, which suddenly sounded much less threatening. "Hold on." The man pulled Frank back a few steps, his grip not slackening for an instant.

A click and the living room lights were snapped on. Frank found himself face-to-face with his attacker: a young man a few years older than himself.

"Frank Hardy," the man said. "Fenton Hardy's oldest son. I've heard a lot about you." He spoke in a clear, unaccented voice and in the light didn't look at all threatening. He had dark hair just like Frank's—a little longer, maybe—and his face seemed somehow familiar. . . .

That was it. Frank snapped his fingers.

"You must be Hugh Nolan's son," he said.

"That's right," the man said. "Ned—Ned Nolan."

He stuck his hand out, and the two of them shook. Frank's other hand went to the back of his neck, to rub some feeling back into the place where Ned had grabbed him.

Ned saw and smiled. "Sorry about that," he said. "But if you walked into your father's apartment after midnight and found somebody tiptoeing around—"

"I understand," Frank said. "You have even more reason to be suspicious today."

Ned frowned. "I don't understand."

"This afternoon, someone tried to kill Chief Peterson."

"What!" Ned's eyes grew wide with surprise.

Just then one of the doors leading into the hall opened, and Joe Hardy stepped through.

His hair was tousled, and he wore only the bottom half of a pair of pajamas.

"Hey," he whispered, glaring at Frank. "Keep it down, would you? Between Dad's snoring, and the racket out here . . ." His voice trailed off as Joe caught sight of Ned.

"This must be your brother Joe," Ned said smoothly.

"Who're you?" Joe asked.

"I'm Ned Nolan," he said. "Hugh's son." He raised his eyebrows. "The owner of your pajama bottoms. Glad to meet you."

Joe laughed slightly, then nodded. "Glad to meet you, too."

Ned turned back to Frank. "Is that why you two are here? Because Chief Peterson was attacked?"

Frank nodded. "Not just us—our father's asleep back there, too."

"Your dad invited us to stay tonight," Joe said. "He's the one who lent me your—uh, pajamas."

"Your father's here as well? Good," Ned said firmly. "The more people around, the better. Especially if one of them is Fenton Hardy." He eyed Frank and Joe questioningly. "But I don't quite understand your role."

"Well—" Frank shrugged. "Joe and I were in town, we read about Daniel Carew getting shot, and we just got involved."

"Just like that? You got involved in a murder

case?" Ned asked. He didn't seem to believe it.

"Sometimes we try to help our father out," Frank replied. He didn't bother to mention the fact that he and Joe had also handled numerous cases on their own.

"Well, I suppose I can understand it, in this instance," Ned said. "I should probably get more interested in this case myself—seeing how deeply it affects my father. Come on," Nolan turned and headed for the kitchen, motioning Frank and Joe to follow. "Let's sit down and talk. There's a fresh bag of potato chips in the bread drawer if you're interested."

Joe smiled his thanks and opened the drawer Ned pointed to.

"So, tell me about this from the beginning."

Frank started by recounting what had happened when he, Joe, and their father had gone to the reading of Moran's will. He had gotten as far as the shouting match between Tommy Poletti and Daniel Carew when Ned interrupted him.

"I was thinking about going with my father that day, but—" Ned shook his head. "I wasn't sure I could be responsible for my actions with all those people there. After they stymied his career—" He broke off in midsentence and looked across the table. "I guess I'm not making much sense, am I?"

Frank and Joe exchanged a quick glance.

"Yes, you are—we heard about what happened to your dad from our father."

"He got a raw deal," Ned said angrily. "You know, after my mom left, he did everything for me. *Everything*. So when those people start calling him names . . ." His voice trailed off.

"For what it's worth, I'm sorry," Frank offered.

"Yeah," Joe said. Frank saw he was about halfway through the big bag of potato chips already.

"Thanks." Ned smiled. "Anyway, that was all a long time ago. So—you were at Moran's house. What do you think? Are both these killings related to that will?"

"Both these attacks—Chief Peterson didn't die," Frank said, correcting him. "And my gut feeling is—yes, they're related, somehow."

"I don't think Tommy Poletti killed Carew," Joe said. "But it does seem like an awfully big coincidence for the two incidents to come so close together—and at this particular time."

Ned was silent for a moment. "All right—if it isn't a coincidence," he asked, "then who's doing it? Which one of the other beneficiaries?"

Frank ticked off the list on his hand. "We started with Hugh Nolan, Johnny Carew, Daniel Carew, Samuel Peterson, Fenton Hardy, Thomas Poletti, and William Delaney. Daniel Carew is dead, Peterson's been attacked—"

"So—Delaney, then," Joe cut in. "It's got to be him."

"I don't know very much about any of those people," Ned said. "But my money's on Johnny Carew."

"You think he'd shoot his own son?" Frank asked dubiously.

Ned shrugged. "No, I suppose not. But from what my father's told me, he seems like the most coldhearted of the bunch. And don't forget," he said, "there could be more than one killer."

"Boy, we've been down this road before." Joe yawned and pushed his chair back from the table. "I think I'm going to hit the sack, guys. See you in the morning."

"Good night, Joe," Ned said.

"Good night." Frank leaned forward over the table. "I think the police are going to get a lot more serious about this case—and its connection to Moran's will—now that Chief Peterson's been poisoned."

"I hope so," Ned said. "Have they found any trace of the man who attacked him?"

Frank shrugged. "I don't know yet, but I doubt it. I probably got a better look at him than anyone, and I don't think I'd recognize him if he walked up to me and shook my hand."

"I suppose that's understandable," Ned

chuckled. "A white shirt isn't exactly an identifying mark."

Frank vainly tried to stifle a yawn. He was falling asleep at the table. "I guess I'm a little tired, too."

"It is late," Ned said, nodding. He cleared the table and led the way back into the living room.

"I think your father has my bed," Ned said, staring down the hall.

"I'll flip you for the sofa," Frank offered.

"That lumpy old thing?" Ned shook his head. "It's all yours." He picked up the sofa's back cushions and arranged them into a makeshift mattress. "I'll make do with these."

"Good night, then." Frank said. He settled back onto the couch—and within minutes was fast asleep.

Frank woke to the smell of frying bacon and the warmth of the sun in his eyes. He showered, dressed, and went into the kitchen.

Hugh Nolan, Ned Nolan, and Frank's father were sitting around the breakfast table, eating, and reading the morning paper. Joe was there as well, but he had pushed his chair about three feet back from the table and was keeping his eyes away from anything that looked like food.

"Morning, everybody."

"Morning, Frank. Help yourself to bacon and eggs," Hugh Nolan said.

Frank nodded his thanks, even though he wasn't particularly hungry yet.

Joe groaned. "It feels like there's a lead weight in my stomach. I don't think I'll ever be hungry again."

"That's why you're not supposed to eat after midnight," Frank said.

"The papers say the police have released Tommy Poletti," Fenton Hardy said, sipping his coffee.

"They finally figured out he's not guilty," Joe said. "I guessed that all along."

"That also means the police are back to square one in their investigation," Fenton said. "Poletti was their only suspect."

"So they don't know any more about who the killer is," Ned said thoughtfully. "Or who might be next."

The doorbell rang.

Frank and his father exchanged a quick glance.

"You expecting anyone, Hugh?" Fenton asked.

Nolan shook his head.

"I'll get it, Dad," Ned said, standing.

"Careful," Fenton Hardy said, instantly serious. Frank noticed the bulge of a shoulder holster beneath his father's sport jacket.

Ned returned with two men, one tall and thin, the other short and stocky. Both were dressed in suits.

"Fenton Hardy? Hugh Nolan?"

Fenton and Hugh stood.

"I'm Detective Martin," the smaller man said, flashing a badge. "This is Detective Stevens. Could we talk to you for a moment? In private?"

Fenton and Hugh led the men to the living room.

"What's this all about?" Ned asked.

Frank shrugged. "Your guess is as good as mine."

When the four men returned a couple of minutes later, Fenton Hardy spoke first.

"These men have just come from a meeting with Chief Peterson and the mayor, boys. The word's come down from the top on this one. It's been decided that the three of us—that is, Hugh Nolan, myself, and Chief Peterson—should disappear for a while." He smiled. "I think I know the perfect place, but we'll have to stop at home first."

"Where's that, Dad?" Frank asked.

Fenton shook his head. "It's better that we keep the location secret," he said. "I'll tell your mother that a case has come up for me but that she should expect you and Joe home tonight."

"But, Dad—" Joe began.

Fenton Hardy shook his head firmly. "No buts. You two get to the library and get to work."

61

"Anytime you're ready," the smaller of the two detectives said. "We'll take you to the chief."

The two older men said their goodbyes—and then, just like that, they were gone.

"I don't like this at all," Frank said, staring out the living room window. On the street below, he saw the four men get into a squad car and drive off.

"Me neither," Joe said.

"What can you do about it?" Ned said. Then, assuming the subject was closed, he switched to another. "So, are you two going to the midtown library today?"

Frank met Joe's eyes, then shook his head.

"We're not leaving the city."

"But your father said—"

Now Frank stared at Ned.

"Whoever's behind the killings—if we assume for the moment that it's one person—he's already managed to infiltrate a precinct station and almost kill the chief of police."

"So?" Ned asked.

"So, what if the killer has a contact inside the police department? There's a great chance he could find our fathers, no matter where they hide." Frank shook his head. "We're not leaving until this killer is caught."

Chapter

8

"ALL RIGHT," Ned said. "What can I do to help?"

"Well," Frank said, "I think a good place to begin is with that list of beneficiaries."

"Motive and opportunity?" Joe asked. That was where they usually began when they had a list of suspects—narrow it down by checking to see who had the motive and who had the opportunity.

"They all have the same motive," Ned pointed out. "Moran's money—ten million dollars. That leaves us with opportunity."

Frank shook his head. "The police are probably doing that right now. And they have a lot more than three people to check out alibis," he said.

"Well—if we can't check opportunity, and they all have the same motive—" Joe smiled suddenly. He saw what Frank was getting at. "They might not all have exactly the same motive, right?"

"Right," his brother replied.

"What do you mean?" Ned asked.

"We're talking about ten million dollars here," Frank said. "Which is admittedly a lot of money. But to, say, Tommy Poletti, it's worth more than to Johnny Carew, who's probably got at least that much already."

"I see," Ned replied. "So what do we do now?"

"We find out how much they're worth," Joe said.

Frank nodded. "Exactly."

"How are we going to do that?"

"I've got a couple of ideas," Frank said. "I'll tell you on the way."

He stood to go.

"On the way where?" Ned asked.

"Just north of the Wall Street area," Frank said.

"Hold on," Joe said. "Let me get a little something to eat."

"I thought you were never going to be hungry again," Frank said.

"Well," Joe said, piling a few slices of bacon and a big spoonful of scrambled eggs onto his plate. "Detective work always gives me an appetite."

* * *

An hour and a half later the three boys were in the waiting room of Vance Johnson's office.

It had been Frank's idea to start digging at the lawyer's for information: impartial information on the people they were most interested in—Billy Delaney and Johnny Carew.

"Mr. Johnson will see you now," Johnson's secretary called out. She led them into the lawyer's office—a large, airy room with high ceilings and a wall of bay windows that looked out onto lower Broadway. Thick, meticulously arranged law volumes lined the floor-to-ceiling bookshelves along one wall. Another wall was dominated by oil portraits of several very distinguished-looking individuals, and the fourth wall was almost completely hidden by a line of massive oak filing cabinets and an old-fashioned water cooler.

It all seemed very proper and respectable. Yet Joe wondered how much of that respectability Johnson had was genuine. After all, he had been Joshua Moran's lawyer.

Johnson was seated behind the massive oak desk, scanning a single sheet of paper. Other than a small stack of papers piled neatly in front of him, his desk was bare. He rose as the three boys entered.

"Mr. Johnson," Frank said, stepping forward, "thank you for agreeing to see us." He nodded in Ned's direction. "This is Ned Nolan."

"Hugh's son, I assume," Johnson said crisply, shaking hands with all of them. "So, I gather this is about Mr. Moran's will."

"That's right," Joe said. "We—"

"Well then, gentlemen." Johnson laid his palms flat on the table and stared directly at them. "My time is valuable—how may I be of service to you?"

Frank seemed slightly taken aback at his formality. Joe, too, knew that was a bad sign, but Johnson's attitude was understandable. He'd probably been grilled by the police more than once during the last few days and obviously wouldn't welcome more questions—especially from three people he probably saw as little more than overly enthusiastic teenagers. Check that, Joe told himself with a glance at Ned, who was past his teens. Two teenagers.

Joe was trying to think of something witty and charming to say when he noticed a large, framed photo. In the photo Johnson was standing with another, much younger man, whom Joe recognized instantly.

"Hey," Joe blurted out. "That's Tommy Poletti."

"Why, yes. That picture was taken the day after the Rose Bowl, the year Tommy was Heisman winner." Johnson nodded. "USC lost, but Tommy was magnificent."

"Five touchdown passes, nineteen straight completions," Joe said. "I remember watching it." Truthfully, he did. It was one of the first football games he'd seen on television—and still one of the best.

"Greatest single game a quarterback has ever had—in my opinion," Johnson said. "But then, Tommy wouldn't settle for doing any less, once he got to the Rose Bowl. That's just the kind of boy he was. Is. I've been close friends with the family for years—worked for his late father for almost four decades."

Joe had a sudden hunch. "The Poletti family—that's how you came to work for Mr. Moran, isn't it? Tommy's relationship with Emily?"

"Why—yes," Johnson said. He seemed somewhat surprised. "When the two of them first started seeing each other in college, Tommy asked me to keep an eye on her family's affairs."

Joe glanced questioningly at Frank, who nodded. Joe knew that that nod meant, Go ahead—it's your show. "Mr. Johnson, we'll try not to waste your time. I'm sure the police have already asked you questions, but we're"—he indicated the three of them—"personally interested in this case in a way that they can't be. It's our fathers' lives that are at stake."

"I see," Johnson said. He crossed to a group of armchairs in the far corner of his office and sat down, indicating that the Hardys and Ned should follow suit.

"I understand your particular closeness to this case, but I'm not sure what I can do to help you."

"Well . . ."

Frank broke in. "We're trying to find out a little more background—financial background—on some of the people Mr. Moran named as beneficiaries. Especially Johnny Carew and Billy Delaney."

Johnson thought for a moment. "Well, as I was telling the police, I know very little about Mr. Carew's activities. I can only make inferences, based on conversations I had with Mr. Moran before his death."

"Every little bit helps," Ned said.

Johnson nodded. "Mr. Moran felt that Mr. Carew's various real-estate holdings were worth upward of one hundred million dollars. His own personal fortune, he estimated at somewhat less than half of that."

"So ten million dollars would still be a lot of money for him," Frank said.

Johnson nodded.

"But would he kill for it?" Joe asked.

"That's the thing about money," Ned put in. "No matter how much you have, you always want more."

"What about Delaney?" Frank asked.

Johnson snorted. "Ten million dollars would be a fortune for him."

"But I thought he'd been running Moran's"—Joe was about to say *gang*, but stopped himself in time—"businesses for him while Moran was in jail."

Johnson nodded. "Running them into the ground."

"I noticed he and Tommy didn't get along too well."

"Nor do he and Emily," Johnson said. "She's particularly uncomfortable having him live in that townhouse with her."

"They live together?"

"It was her father's request. But now that he's gone—well, I expect Delaney will be moving out shortly."

"How does she feel about all this—the killing, I mean?"

Johnson sighed deeply. "She's quite upset. She has me working to find a way to invalidate her father's will."

Joe was surprised. "Why? Won't that affect her share of the estate?"

"Perhaps," Johnson said. "That's uncertain. But she really has very little interest in that money, if you can believe it."

"I do find it a little hard to believe," Ned said quietly.

Johnson glowered at him. "Emily wants only to marry Tommy, and she would just as soon never see a penny of her father's wealth. She was never close to him."

Joe decided he'd bet money that Johnson had gotten involved with Joshua Moran only at Tommy Poletti's prompting—and quite reluctantly, at that.

"What do you think?" Frank asked. "Is there a chance of getting Moran's will set aside?"

"I hadn't thought so until recently. However, I think I may have found something. . . ." He pulled out a manila folder.

"Ah, yes," Johnson said, thumbing through the pages. "It occurred to me that if we can prove that Mr. Moran lacked testamentary capacity at the time he made out his will, we may be able to have the entire document declared void."

"Testamentary capacity—you mean, whether or not he was in his right mind?" Ned asked.

"Exactly," Johnson replied.

"Your ten-thirty is here, Mr. Johnson," his secretary said over the intercom.

"Thank you, Mrs. Hunter. I'm afraid that's all the time I can spare, boys. I hope I've been of some help."

"You have, Mr. Johnson," Joe assured him. "And thanks."

They shook hands all around, and Johnson promised to keep them up-to-date on his efforts to have Moran's will nullified.

Back down on the street, they talked about the information the lawyer had given them.

"He had a lot to say," Ned said. "Especially after you recognized that picture, Joe."

"True," the younger Hardy replied. "It seems to me that he's anxious to put this whole affair behind him."

"One thing seems certain," Ned said. "From what he told us, Delaney needs the money a lot more than Carew."

"With Josh Moran dead, he could begin to lose control of his gang," Joe said. "Add that to his financial problems—"

"And you get a prime suspect," Ned said, finishing Joe's thought. "Delaney could be our man."

"Johnson doesn't like Delaney very much, though," Frank said thoughtfully. "We have to consider the possibility he's not giving us entirely accurate information."

"That's true," Joe admitted. "And Delaney can't be the actual killer—he's a lot bigger than the man I ran into in the hospital."

"On the other hand, Delaney could have hired someone to do that," Ned suggested.

Frank nodded. "I think it's worth our paying Mr. Delaney a little visit."

To their surprise, Delaney himself answered the door at the Moran brownstone.

"Yeah?"

He obviously wasn't in a good mood. It didn't make his face, which Joe had remembered as rather homely, any more attractive. But Joe had forgotten the man was so big.

"This'll just take a second, sir," Joe said. He slid his foot inside the door so Delaney couldn't slam it on him.

"It'll take less than that, sonny," Delaney said. "You're Hardy's kid, ain't you? What're you doing, nosing around here?" He tried to shut the door and failed because Joe's foot was in the way.

"We just have a few questions—" Frank began, moving up next to Joe.

"Trouble, boss?" Another man came to the door behind Delaney. Joe recognized him as one of the mob who'd gathered around Delaney at the reading of the will.

The newcomer saw Joe, then Frank, and his eyes widened.

"It's the Hardy kids, boss," the man said. "Both of them."

"You two got a lot of nerve, showing your faces around here," Delaney continued.

Without warning, Delaney's arm shot out and grabbed Joe's coat collar. Delaney began dragging him forward, as easily as if he were a rag doll. The man was incredibly strong.

Joe realized suddenly that he might be in a lot of trouble.

"I guess we're going to have to teach you

some manners, smart guy,'' Delaney said. By now, he had pulled Joe so close that their noses were almost touching.

"Yeah,'' the other man chimed in menacingly. His eyes never left Frank as he slowly moved in on him. "Starting now. Right now."

Chapter

9

"Mr. Delaney, you don't need to do this,"
Frank began, sidestepping to throw his would-
be assailant off balance. The man behind Delaney couldn't maneuver close enough to
Frank to grab him now.

"I don't have to," Delaney growled. "But I
want to." He drew his arm back as if he was
going to swing at Joe.

"Let him go, Mr. Delaney," Ned said, moving into the space Frank had left.

Delaney snorted. "Who are you?"

"Ned Nolan—and I'm telling you—"

"Hugh Nolan's kid? That weasel?" Delaney
barked out a laugh. "If you're anything like
your old man, I could just—"

Things happened fast then. There was a flash
of movement, and suddenly Delaney wasn't

holding Joe anymore. He was holding his own hands and rubbing them.

"Watch what you do to my friends," Ned said. "And especially watch what you say about my father."

"Oh," Delaney said, looking up. "So you want to play rough." He stepped forward, and swung at Ned. Frank could feel the air move with the force of his blow, which was surprisingly fast for a man of his size. Ned ducked it easily and threw a punch of his own. The big man staggered on his feet, gasping for breath.

"That's it, pal." Delaney's hood moved forward with a drawn gun. "Beat it."

Frank held both his hands up and stepped in front of Ned again. "All right, things got a little out of hand, but—"

"I said beat it!" Delaney's hood slammed the door in his face, leaving the three of them standing on the stoop.

"That settles that," Frank said.

"Wow," Joe said, staring at Ned. "What did you do to Delaney?"

"Taught him some manners, I expect," Ned said, smiling. He laid an arm on Joe's shoulder. "Are you all right?"

"Yeah, I'm fine," Joe said. He paused a moment. "You didn't have to do that, Ned."

"It was my pleasure."

"No, Ned," Frank said quietly. "Joe means you shouldn't have done that."

Ned turned to face him, a surprised look on his face.

"You cost us a chance to talk to Delaney," Frank said.

"What should I have done, Frank? Let him strangle your brother?"

Joe shook his head. "He wouldn't have strangled me."

"Really? We're talking about the man who probably killed Daniel Carew—and tried to kill Chief Peterson," Ned said coldly. "Need I point out that your father—or mine—could be next?"

"We don't know that Delaney killed any-one," Frank said. "Ned, you can't let your emotions run away with you if—"

"If I'm going to be a detective, is that it?"

The two of them stood silently staring at each other.

"Yes," Frank said finally.

"Well, then maybe I shouldn't be a detective," Ned said angrily. "I'll leave the field to you two."

"Ned, wait." Joe grabbed his arm. "You don't have to—"

Ned threw Joe's grip off and stalked off without looking back.

"Let him go," Frank told his brother. "He just needs to cool off."

They stood on the bottom step of Delaney's brownstone, staring after him.

"Hey!"

Frank turned. The voice belonged to Delaney's friend, the man who'd pulled the gun on them. He was leaning out the front door of the townhouse, glaring down at them.

"Didn't I tell you guys to beat it?"

Joe turned toward him angrily, but Frank laid a hand on his shoulder before he could speak.

"We're on our way," he said, pulling Joe away. "We're not going to get anything accomplished here, that's for sure," he muttered under his breath.

"So what's next?"

Frank looked at his watch. It was almost one o'clock. "Well—there is one thing we do have to do this afternoon."

"What's that?"

"Our research at the library."

Joe groaned.

Joe actually did have a very productive afternoon at the library.

He finished his work early and decided to look into the incident that seemed to be at the heart of the case. He watched microfilms of newspaper articles from twenty years ago, when the Jefferson Heights townhouses had been built—when that terrible fire, which killed twelve people, had taken place.

It was all there, just as his father had told

them. And the more Joe read, the more suspicious that fire looked. He dug back farther, searching for more information on the deal that had been struck to tear down and "renovate" the Jefferson Heights area.

The earliest mention he found came complete with pictures of Josh Moran himself. One showed Moran at city hall, during discussions regarding the Jefferson Heights project. The photographer had caught Moran in midsentence, making a point. He was probably in his early forties then—a handsome man, with jet black hair and precise, angular features, which his daughter Emily had clearly inherited.

Joe recognized few other people in the picture, identified as city officials, including the then-mayor of New York, a few police officers—

His heart stopped.

He moved the viewer in closer, enlarging the photographed image.

There, directly behind Moran, his face partially obscured by that man's arm, was Hugh Nolan. His presence there was proof of nothing, of course, but Nolan was smiling in the picture, and Joe got the sense that he and Moran were connected in some way.

Suddenly he wasn't sure Ned's father had gotten a raw deal after all. He and Moran clearly knew each other.

He looked through a few more articles on

the project but found nothing else of interest. After returning the microfilms, he found Frank and sat down to tell him about his afternoon's work.

"So Hugh Nolan may be a suspect, too," Frank said thoughtfully. "Which leaves us with the question of how this all fits together. It's got to relate back to what happened twenty years ago."

"It seems pretty obvious to me," Joe said. "Moran took the fall for Carew, so he was mad at him. He was mad at Dad and Chief Peterson for putting him away, and he came up with a very creative way of getting back at all of them."

"But what about Tommy and Hugh?" Frank asked. "And who's doing the killings now—and why?"

Joe shrugged. "That I can't help you with."

"But that's what we've got to figure out," Frank said. "And we've got to find someplace else to do our figuring, I guess. We're probably not going to be too welcome at the Nolans' anymore."

But when they returned to the Nolans' apartment to return the keys Hugh had given them, they found a note waiting for them.

Frank and Joe,
    Sorry I got so angry with you earlier. Please feel free to stay and use the apart-

ment. I may be out late tonight, but I'll catch up with you tomorrow.

Ned

"Well," Joe said, slumping down on the couch. "That's good. At least we have a base of operations. So, what do we do tonight?"

"Well . . ." Frank sat down next to him. "We can't go back and see Delaney—"

"Or Emily, since she lives in the same place." Joe thought a moment. "Maybe we should try Johnny Carew."

Frank shook his head. "How about we talk to a friendly face this time?"

"Whom did you have in mind?"

"Tommy Poletti."

Joe nodded. "That's a good idea. But how are we going to find him? I don't expect a former Heisman trophy winner has a listed address."

"I know where he lives," Frank said. "I caught a glimpse of the police file on him when we went to see Chief Peterson that first time."

"He's got a record?" Joe asked, clearly upset. "Why? What for?"

"I couldn't see that part of the file," Frank said.

Joe shook his head. "I don't believe it."

"You can ask him about it when we get there, then," Frank said, grabbing his coat. "Come on."

"Where're we going? Where does he live?"

"Where everybody connected with this case seems to live," Frank replied. "Brooklyn."

After grabbing a bite to eat, the brothers took the subway back to Brooklyn. They got off at the first stop, and from there it was just a five-minute walk to Poletti's apartment.

Tommy lived right next to the Brooklyn Bridge, in a beautiful neighborhood of brownstones. As they turned onto his block, a figure emerged from one of the brownstones ahead of them and walked out onto the street. A tall, dark man who looked in both directions before heading directly toward them.

It was Tommy Poletti. Frank pretended not to notice him.

"Wait," Joe said. "That's him. Let's catch up and—"

"No," Frank said, grabbing hold of his brother's arm and dragging him across the street. "He obviously doesn't want to be followed."

"So?" Joe asked.

"So let's see where he's going before we announce ourselves."

"All right," Joe said reluctantly. "We'll tail him for a while."

Frank studied his brother closely. Was Joe letting his admiration for Poletti cloud his judgment? He hoped not.

Frank began tailing Poletti, keeping on the

opposite side of the street and half a block behind the man. Joe fell back a half block behind his brother. As Frank walked, he pulled a wool ski cap out of his pocket and put it on. Whenever he and Joe did a two-man tail, they used the hat, or something like it, as a signal. If Frank felt the quarry was getting suspicious of him, he'd take off the cap and fall back, letting Joe pick up the man's trail. His brother would then follow the same procedure.

But in this case, all their precautions turned out to be unnecessary. For Poletti walked straight across the Brooklyn Bridge at such a brisk pace that Frank had trouble keeping up with him. Poletti was clearly on some kind of schedule—he kept checking his watch—and didn't even look back once. Halfway across the bridge, Joe caught up with Frank.

"He's sure in a hurry," Joe said, breathing heavily.

"To go where?"

"Maybe this is how he keeps in shape," Joe suggested with a grin. "This feels like a waste of time to me, Frank."

Frank shook his head. "Let's just see how it develops before we do anything."

Joe nodded resignedly and fell back behind Frank again.

Poletti continued his rapid pace as he left the bridge and crossed into Manhattan. He strode by City Hall and continued north, past all the government buildings. Just before Chinatown, Poletti took a left and headed west, toward the Hudson River. Within a few minutes Frank was trailing the man through a maze of four- and five-story commercial buildings in an old manufacturing district.

Then Poletti stopped. In the middle of the block ahead of him a long line of limousines was parked, and a crowd of people were gathered at the entrance to a building.

Frank crossed to the other side of the street and continued walking, past Poletti and directly toward the crowd. As he passed them, he heard an insistent, thudding beat coming from inside the door. And a small sign above the door, white letters on a black background, read simply Cosmos.

Suddenly he felt very foolish. The place was a nightclub. Joe had been right after all. Poletti was simply going out, probably meeting someone here.

Another limousine pulled up in front of the club, and an older man emerged from the driver's seat. He walked around the car, opened the rear passenger door—and Billy Delaney stepped out.

The two doormen immediately parted the crowd to let Delaney's men and Delaney pass through the entrance to the club.

Was this what Poletti had been waiting for? As soon as Delaney entered the club, Tommy started walking again—this time past the entrance, toward the end of the block.

Frank shook his head. Why, if Poletti had come here to meet Delaney, wasn't he going inside?

Frank could think of only one reason.

Poletti hadn't come here to meet the man. He'd come here to kill him.

Chapter

10

FRANK HAD TO MAKE a quick decision—should he follow Poletti, or see what Delaney was up to inside the club?

As he thought about it, he decided he didn't have much choice. Poletti may have been preoccupied, but Frank had walked directly past him. He must have been seen—and it would look too suspicious if Poletti saw him again.

Frank took off his ski cap and joined the crowd waiting to get into Cosmos. As he pushed toward the front of the mob, he saw Joe race down the corner after Poletti.

"Cover charge is twenty dollars tonight, kid." Frank looked up to find one of the doormen, a large black man with a shaved head, studying him from behind the roped-off entrance to the club. "And I'm going to need some ID—with a picture."

Frank groaned. ID—he'd forgotten all about it. In New York, you had to be twenty-one to get into the clubs. Now what was he going to do?

Improvise.

"I just came from in there," Frank began, "and I think I left my wallet inside—"

"Hey, look, kid," the bouncer said, turning his full attention to Frank. "If you don't have an ID, step out of the way." The man folded his arms across his chest and glowered threateningly at him.

"Never mind," Frank said, turning away. Now what was he going to do? He had to get inside to find out what Delaney was doing—and if necessary, warn him that Poletti was after him.

He trudged away from the club, so deep in thought that he almost missed the iron fence blocking an alleyway that ran right next to the club. He took a quick look around. The only people on the street were those at the entrance to Cosmos, and the only thing on their minds was getting into the club.

Taking a deep breath, Frank jumped up, caught the top of the fence, and carefully boosted himself up and over the spikes on top. He jumped, bending his knees to land quietly on the other side.

A door from the club was pushed out into the alley just then.

Frank dropped to the ground and lay still.

A man, wearing a white apron over a plain white T-shirt, stepped through the door carrying a large trash bag in each hand. Whistling happily, he dropped the bags in the alley next to a pile of about twenty others, wiped his hands, and went back inside. The door swung shut behind him.

Frank got up slowly and dusted himself off. This must be my lucky day, he said to himself.

He was right. The door was unlocked—and when Frank cracked it slightly, he heard whistling and the muffled thump of noise from the club.

He pulled the door open a hair farther and peered in.

The man he had seen take out the trash was at a sink off to the left, about twenty feet away. His back was to Frank, and he was scrubbing a large pot and singing along with the music coming from inside the club.

Directly opposite Frank was a set of double doors with small square windows. Through them, he could see pulsing lights.

Frank eased the door back and slid inside. He strode quickly and quietly toward those lights, taking off his jacket as he walked.

Walking into the club was like being on the

fifty-yard line during the Super Bowl halftime show.

The first thing that hit him was the music—the song playing had a thudding, droning, synthesized beat and was turned up so loud he could actually feel the thump of the bass drum in the pit of his stomach. Lights flashed on and off, making the white shirt he was wearing change colors, from orange to green to red—and back to orange again.

Inside, Cosmos was one huge round room, broken up into different levels with what looked almost like construction scaffolding. And standing on that scaffolding were some of the strangest looking and most strangely dressed people he had ever seen.

In the center of the room was an enormous, sunken dance floor. Across the room, almost directly opposite Frank, was a horseshoe-shaped bar.

In the crowd at the bar, Frank saw the man who'd pulled the gun on them at Delaney's.

As Frank watched, he took two bottles of what looked like champagne from the bartender and headed up some metal stairs toward the rear of the club.

Frank circled around the dance floor and followed the guy up the stairs. They seemed to go on forever, leading Frank away from the club. As Frank got closer to the top, the noise from below faded, and the stairs dead-ended on a large landing at a plain gray metal door.

Private, it read. No Admittance.

Frank tested the knob. It turned silently in his hand. He nudged the door open slightly and risked a quick peek behind it.

He caught a glimpse of a large, comfortable-looking room, with wood paneling, skylights, and a desk on the far wall. Seated on a large couch in the center of the room was Johnny Carew, smoking a cigar. Two men in turtlenecks and dark sport coats stood behind the couch, flanking him. Billy Delaney sat with his back to Frank on a chair in front of the couch; the two men he'd brought with him to the club sat in chairs behind him.

Frank eased the door back, leaving it ajar an inch, his ear up against it, and listened.

"And I want to assure you I had nothing to do with Daniel's death." That was Delaney speaking.

"If I thought for a moment you had killed him," Carew said, his voice clear and ringing, "you would have been dead within an hour, Billy."

"Maybe," Delaney said. "And maybe if you'd come gunning for me, you'd have been the one to end up dead."

There was an uncomfortable few seconds of silence. Even through the door, Frank could sense the two glaring at each other, each waiting for the other to back down.

Delaney cracked first.

"Look, Johnny, there's no sense in *our* fighting," Delaney said. "Especially with Emily trying to have the whole will nullified. You know that'll turn it into a free-for-all."

Carew still said nothing.

"The only way to make sure we keep control of the situation is if you let me remain in charge of Josh's concerns," Delaney continued. "I'll see you get a percentage, of course."

"A percentage?" Carew demanded loudly. Frank heard the scrape of a chair against the floor. "All right, I'll take a percentage. How about one hundred percent?"

"Johnny, you have to negotiate with me," Delaney replied.

"I don't have to do nothing," Carew said. "You've got no power, Billy. It all dried up and blew away when Josh Moran died. You don't even have Emily Moran to count on. So I'll take back the territory Josh stole from me, sure—but I won't give you anything for it."

Delaney's voice hardened. "Then maybe we should be talking about fighting, Johnny. Because I won't—"

Suddenly there was a sharp *crack!*—followed instantly by the tinkle of shattering glass.

Frank risked another peek inside.

Four of the men in the room had drawn guns. All of them were staring straight up at a sky-light.

And on the floor, lying motionless at Johnny Carew's feet, was Billy Delaney.

Chapter

11

JOE TRAILED TOMMY POLETTI around the block to an abandoned building, his thoughts paralleling Frank's. He'd watched Delaney arrive at the club, and Poletti had obviously timed his arrival to coincide with that of Josh Moran's former lieutenant.

The big question was *why?*

Huge letters painted on the side of the building, now long since faded, announced it as the home of Schickelman Importers—New York's Largest. But Schickelman, whoever he had been, was obviously long gone, along with his importing business. Now as Joe watched Poletti lift himself up and over the sill of a window and disappear into the building, he grew even more suspicious. He hoped his suspicions would turn out to be misplaced.

Giving the man a few seconds' lead, Joe

boosted himself up and in, landing in a pitch-black space.

When his eyes adjusted to the small amount of light filtering through the filthy windows, he saw that the inside of the former warehouse had been completely gutted. Toward the back, he just made out Poletti climbing the only staircase. Joe stole across the vast floor, his feet scratching the gritty dirt against the hardwood. He climbed up after Poletti and found himself on the roof of the building itself.

He scanned the adjoining rooftops. Nothing. There was no sign of Tommy Poletti. Had the man managed to slip behind him? Joe turned to head back down into the warehouse.

Then a sudden, all-too-familiar crack echoed behind him. The crack of a gunshot.

Joe whirled. The sound had come from off to his left. And running straight toward him from that direction was Tommy Poletti.

Joe ducked behind a chimney. As Poletti ran even with him, Joe tackled the former football player.

They rolled over on the hard rooftop together. Poletti might not have played football for several years, but he was still in excellent shape—beneath the jacket he was wearing, the man was solid muscle.

He threw Joe off easily and sprang to his feet.

"What did you do?" Joe asked shakily, also

standing up. He couldn't believe it. Poletti was the killer after all. "Where's the gun?"

"Gun? What are you talking about?" Poletti was furious. "What did you tackle me for?"

"That gunshot," Joe said, his voice shaking. "Who did you kill?"

"Kill? Are you nuts?" Poletti said. He looked at Joe for the first time. "Hey—you're the Hardy kid. You were at the reading of the will, weren't you?"

"That's right," Joe said. "What are you doing here?"

"I could ask you the same thing," Poletti said.

"I'm following you," Joe said. "And I just heard a gunshot and saw you running away—"

"I don't have to tell you what I'm doing here," Poletti said defensively.

"Maybe not," Joe said, unable to keep the bitterness out of his voice. "But you'll have to tell the cops."

"Cops?" Poletti shook his head. "Oh, no, I'm not talking to any more cops."

"I'll tell them about this," Joe said fiercely. "Unless you kill me, too."

"All right," Poletti said, shaking his head. "But you're wrong about this, kid."

"Maybe I am," Joe said, but he didn't believe it. As far as he was concerned, the evidence was doing all the talking.

* * *

For what seemed like forever, Frank watched as no one in Carew's office moved.

Finally one of Delaney's men bent over his boss's body.

"He's dead," the man announced.

"The shot came from up there," Carew said, pointing up at the skylight. He turned to a couple of his men.

"Monk, Moses, you two check it out."

Both nodded and turned toward the door.

Frank started to ease the door shut, preparing to step away from it and rush back down the stairs.

"Hey—what are you doing up here?"

Frank turned. A lean, sharply dressed man with straight blond hair was standing a few feet to the side of him, glaring.

"I guess I got lost," Frank said. He smiled and shrugged.

The man wasn't having any of it. "And I guess you just decided to listen in to what Mr. Carew was saying, is that it?" He clenched his hands into fists. "We'll see what he has to say about this."

Frank shook his head slowly and pretended to look scared. "Please," Frank said. "Don't—"

When the man was just a foot away, Frank sprang into action. Backing up, Frank grabbed the stair railing with both hands. He kicked at the man approaching him, slamming both feet into his chest. The man tumbled back, stunned.

Frank turned and tore down the stairway.

"Hey! Stop that guy!"

At the next landing another man was standing, blocking the stairs going down. He made a snatch at Frank, arms wide. Frank ducked and caught the man in the side with his elbow as the man lunged past. Frank bolted down the next flight of stairs, to the next landing—the one closest to the club floor.

This landing was packed with people, talking and staring down at the dance floor below. The stairs leading down were so crowded that it would take him a full five minutes to travel that one flight, and his pursuers would be all over him by then.

As he was figuring out how to negotiate his way down, a man forced his way up through the crowd on the stairs to the landing. It was the bouncer from the front door. When he caught sight of Frank, he did a double take.

Clearly the man remembered Frank from earlier. Anger darkened his face, and he began heading straight for Frank, parting the crowd between them with no more effort than he would have expended wading through a creek.

Frank looked up and behind him. The two men he'd fought with earlier were down the stairs, closing on him.

He pushed his way to the edge of the landing and looked out over the railing and down the scaffolding to the dance floor a good twenty feet below him.

It was too far to jump, so he swung over the railing and began climbing down the scaffolding, hand over hand, toward the floor.

It was actually an easy climb—there were plenty of handholds and joints in the scaffolding where he could rest his feet. He got about halfway down before he looked up to check on his pursuers.

Carew's men were leaning over the railing, yelling. But the music was so loud, no one on the dance floor could hear them. One of them drew a gun, but the bouncer grabbed his arm, and shook his head. Then Frank couldn't see them anymore—they had disappeared from the railing.

He guessed they were going to try to beat him down the stairs to the dance floor.

Redoubling his efforts to reach bottom quickly, Frank noticed that a lot of people were now aware of him. Several had even stopped what they were doing to look up at him. As he swung to the floor, many of them started applauding.

So much for trying to be inconspicuous, Frank thought.

"Cool, man," one dancer said. "I never saw anybody climb up that high before."

"Or down," the girl with him said. "That was really neat."

Frank nodded, breathing heavily. The crowd blocked his view of the staircase, but he was certain he'd beaten Carew's men down. Now to get out of there . . .

He began threading his way through the crowded dance floor. But it was jam-packed with people, and it was impossible to move very fast. By the time he reached its edge, he knew that whatever time he'd picked up on Carew's men was lost. His only hope was that he'd lost them in the crowd.

He broke through—and suddenly, right in front of him, was the entrance to the club.

The bouncer was standing directly in front of it, looking right at him.

Frank scanned the room desperately. The double doors he'd entered from the kitchen—

One of the men he'd fought on the stairs was standing there, blocking that exit, too. Frank was trapped.

There was no way out. No way at all.

Chapter

12

FRANK DECIDED to head for the front door. It was closest to him, and if he was lucky, the bouncer wasn't on Carew's payroll. . . .

The bouncer saw him coming and grinned.

Then Frank broke into a grin of his own.

Detective Mike Lewis was standing at the door, just behind the bouncer. Joe was just behind Lewis. Frank didn't know what either of them was doing there, and at the moment he didn't care.

Frank walked straight toward the front door as Lewis reached up and tapped the smiling bouncer on the shoulder.

He turned.

"Detective Mike Lewis, NYPD," he said. "Mind if we come in?"

"This guy's really keen on getting ID, Detective Lewis," Frank said. "Better show him yours."

Lewis flashed his badge.

The bouncer growled in frustration and motioned the detective forward.

"We found the gun right behind the skylight—up on the roof," a uniformed officer said, handing a revolver to Lewis. Twenty minutes had passed, and the detective, several uniformed officers, and Frank and Joe were gathered on the street outside Cosmos. Delaney's body had already been taken away by an ambulance. Carew was inside the club, refusing to answer any questions.

"And that's where you say you traced Poletti to?" the detective asked Joe. Lewis, along with a squad car, had been assigned to watch Johnny Carew—and so he had been in perfect position to grab Joe and Tommy Poletti after the shot had been fired. They'd been expecting this "summit" between Carew and Delaney for months, Lewis explained.

"That's right," his brother nodded glumly. "Although I didn't actually see him fire it."

"Of course he didn't!" Poletti shouted. "Because I didn't have anything to do with this!"

"Maybe you'd better wait till your lawyer gets here before saying anything, Tommy," Lewis said, not without a touch of sympathy in his voice.

"I don't need any lawyer," Poletti said fiercely. "Why would I have come with the kid"—he indicated Joe—"so willingly if I shot Delaney, anyway? Huh? Answer that!"

Lewis shook his head. "That's not my job, I'm afraid." He opened the rear door of the squad car. "My job is to get you downtown now."

Poletti exhaled and climbed in the back-seat—but not before shooting Joe an angry look.

"I'll let you know what happens," Lewis said.

Lewis nodded. "Good work, boys," he said.

"Yeah—" Joe stood shaking his head as the police car drove off. Right then he didn't feel as if he'd just done anything that anyone would call "good work."

"Well, I'm just not sure, that's all," Frank said. It was morning and he was sitting in the Nolans' living room, discussing the case with Ned and Joe. Delaney's killing had happened too late to make the morning papers, but the news had been all over the radio.

"How can you not be sure, Frank?" Ned asked. "They've got the murder weapon, and the killer."

"Think, though," Frank said. "Why? Why would Tommy Poletti kill to increase his share of ten million dollars when he's going to get a lot more than that once he marries Emily Moran?''

''Murderers don't reason that way,'' Ned said firmly. ''Or maybe he's not going to marry Emily—I don't know. What I do know is that this seems to be over. We can tell our fathers to come home now.''

The phone rang. Ned answered it.

''It's for either of you,'' he said, holding out the receiver.

''I'll take it,'' Frank said. He grabbed the receiver.

''This is Frank Hardy.''

''Frank, this is Detective Lewis. Just thought you and your brother would want to know. We ran a ballistics test on that gun. It's the same one that killed Daniel Carew.'' Lewis was silent a moment. ''We're charging Tommy Poletti with murder one.''

''You're sure?'' Frank asked.

''Sure as we can get without a confession.''

Frank sighed. ''All right—thanks.''

He hung up the phone and turned to his brother, who'd been unusually quiet all morning. The news of Poletti's guilt had hit him pretty hard.

''They say they're going to charge Poletti,'' Frank told them.

''It's over, then,'' Joe said.

''I don't think so,'' Frank replied firmly. ''What about this, Joe? Johnson said Emily

Moran had asked him to find a way to invalidate the will—don't you think Poletti knew about that? Why would he risk his neck killing Carew and Delaney when the whole document might be nullified?"

"It's over, Frank—face it," Joe repeated. "We're not going to find some magic clue the police overlooked this time."

"I'm not looking for any magic clue," Frank said. "I'm looking for the truth—and if you're going to sit here moping all day, I guess I'll have to look myself." He stood up and grabbed his coat.

Joe didn't move.

"I'm going to try to talk to Emily Moran," Frank said. Without another word, he stalked to the front door and threw it open. He sucked in air and gave a low whistle.

Framed in the doorway were two men. Carew's goons. He recognized one of them from the club.

"Oh," the man said, smiling. "Now this is a pleasure we didn't anticipate." He drew a gun with one hand, and with the other he roughly shoved Frank back into the apartment.

"I've been looking all over town for you—and you show up here." He pointed his gun at Frank. "I guess this is going to be my lucky day."

Chapter

13

HIS COMPANION STEPPED IN behind him and shut the door.

"So you're Ned Nolan," the man said to Frank.

"No, I'm Ned Nolan." Ned and Joe had appeared in the arch between the hall and the living room. "What's going on here?"

"Frank, who is this guy?" Joe asked.

"I'm his fairy godmother," the man said. "It don't matter who I am. What matters is this," he said, flicking his gun. He motioned Ned and Joe toward the door. "Let's go, all three of you."

Joe shrugged and stepped forward, then suddenly stopped and planted his feet. He swung his elbow to the side and knocked the goon's gun out of his hand.

In a flash his hand was inches from picking it up. He stopped half bent over when he heard the unmistakable sound of a trigger being cocked.

Joe looked up. The second gunman had a revolver to Ned's head.

"Leave the gun alone," the man said simply.

Joe had no choice. He stepped back.

"One more trick like that, kid," the first guy said, bending over to pick up his revolver, "and you'll be staying here—permanently. Now let's go."

The three of them were taken back to Cosmos—and to the office Frank had seen the previous evening. Johnny Carew was there himself, waiting.

"What's going on, Terry?" Carew asked the man who'd brought them there.

"This"—he waved his gun at Ned—"is Nolan's son. And this"—he indicated Frank—"is that punk who was in here last night. I don't know who the other one is."

"Ah, but I do," Carew said, carefully scrutinizing first Frank, then Joe. "You're Hardy's two boys, aren't you?"

"That's right," Frank said.

"Playing detective, are you? Hope to follow in your father's footsteps?" Carew asked the question with a smile, but there was underlying malice to his words.

"Why are we here?" Joe demanded.

"Feisty, eh? I like that." Carew laughed and sat down behind his desk. "All right, I'll tell you."

"It has to do with Josh Moran's will, doesn't it?" Frank asked.

"It does at that," Carew nodded. "Moran's will—and my son's death." He silently stared off into space for a moment. When he began talking again, his voice was lower, more intense.

"I had a funny thought last night, when the police were hounding me with questions about Billy Delaney." He lifted his gaze to Frank's. "I was thinking how funny it would be if one of the people the police would never think of questioning—one of the 'good guys'—had actually killed my son. Somebody who could really use Josh Moran's money—somebody like Hugh Nolan, for instance, or maybe even Fenton Hardy.

"So I sent Terry and Monk"—he nodded at the men standing guard at the door—"to find those two and bring them here for a little talk. Instead, I got you."

He nodded to Terry, who moved forward and laid a hand on Frank's shoulder and guided him, none too gently, into a chair in front of Carew's desk. Joe and Ned were also marched over and made to sit in chairs next to Frank.

"So," Carew asked, folding his hands and

leaning forward on his desk. "Where are they?"

"We don't know," Frank said.

"Come now—that won't do," Carew said, shaking his head. "Where are they?"

"He just told you," Ned said. "We really don't know. Besides, haven't you been paying attention? The police have your son's killer—and Delaney's—in custody. Tommy Poletti."

Carew waved a hand in dismissal. "That's a load of garbage."

Joe did a double take. "You don't think Poletti killed your son?"

Carew shook his head. "Tommy Poletti? A killer? Never. The police will figure that out soon enough. If they don't, they're even bigger fools than I thought."

Frank leaned back in his chair and exchanged a look with Joe.

"I don't know where my father is," Frank said. "That's the truth. But you're wrong if you think he's had anything to do with the killings."

"Your father's a man of principle—is that it? Well, we're talking about ten million dollars here, sonny," Carew said. "That much money buys a lot of principles."

"Not my father's," Frank said firmly.

"Or mine," Ned added.

At that, Carew laughed harshly. "Hugh Nolan? Not interested in money? You don't know him very well—do you, sonny?''

"What do you mean by that?'' Ned asked angrily, rising from his chair. He was upset enough to attack Carew with his bare hands.

The gang lord studied Ned calmly for a second, then shook his head. "Never mind. All right, you say you don't know where your fathers are. I'll accept that—for now.'' Now Carew looked directly at Frank. "But the next time you want to play detective, you play with someone else, okay?''

"We don't play at being detectives, Mr. Carew,'' Frank said calmly. "Especially where our father's life is concerned.''

"And I don't play around when it comes to whoever killed my son!'' Carew slammed his fist down on the desk. "You make sure you understand that.''

He glowered at Frank for a moment, then snapped his fingers. "Get them out of here.''

Terry and Monk escorted them down to the street.

"Carew doesn't think Poletti did it either,'' Joe said, more to himself than anyone else. "Guess I'm beginning to believe the killer is still on the loose.''

"I told you,'' Frank said. "I'm going to see Emily Moran. You two coming?''

Joe grinned. "You bet. Ned?''

Ned shook his head slowly. "No, I don't

think so." He was still clearly upset by Carew's accusation—an accusation Joe decided might be right after his discovery in the library.

But in Ned's mind they were still just doubts—and Joe didn't want to upset Ned any further without real proof.

"Well, we'll see you back at the apartment later," Frank said. "Come on, Joe—let's go play detective."

This time, their reception at Emily's was slightly more pleasant. Emily Moran, even though she looked even more tired and upset than the last time they'd seen her, was happy to talk with them.

"We appreciate your taking the time to see us, Ms. Moran—especially today," Joe said. Delaney's death had apparently enabled Emily to rid herself of the man's entourage as well. The house seemed deserted except for the three of them.

She nodded distractedly. "Yes, I talked to Vance, and he said you were trying to find the killer." She forced a grin. "Besides, there's not much else I can do right now. The police are questioning Tommy again."

"I hope you don't think this is rude," Joe began, "but—why did your father put Tommy Poletti into his will?"

"Dad didn't exactly like Tommy," Emily said. "He was in jail of course when I first met

Tommy, and he never approved of him. I think my dad wanted me to see someone who could help run his business." She stopped suddenly to look at her watch. "The police are supposed to call me when they're finished questioning him," she said, apologizing.

"They take a long time sometimes," Joe offered sympathetically.

"Don't I know it," Emily said, smiling. "You're talking to Josh Moran's daughter, after all." It was the first time Joe had seen her genuinely amused at something, and it made her look about five years younger.

Suddenly Joe wanted very much for Tommy Poletti to be proven innocent.

"I just wish there was something I could do to help him," Emily continued.

"There may be," Frank said. "Announce that you've found a way to have your father's will nullified."

Emily looked confused. "How will that help Tommy?"

Joe explained. "By flushing out the real killer."

"So you don't think Tommy's guilty?" Emily asked, her eyes glistening.

Frank and Joe both shook their heads. "No," Joe said.

"All right," she nodded firmly. "Give me a minute—I'll get my coat. Then we'll go talk to Vance to have him make the announcement."

It was just after two o'clock when they reached Johnson's office. The place was completely deserted.

"That's strange," Frank said, shaking his head. "I wonder where everybody is."

"Out to lunch?" Joe suggested.

"I don't think so," Frank said. "Look." He pointed at a half-eaten sandwich lying on the secretary's desk. Next to the sandwich, her computer was still running.

The brothers exchanged a puzzled glance.

Emily Moran crossed to Johnson's office door and rapped on it loudly.

"Nobody in there either," she said.

"I guess we come back later," Frank said. He turned to go.

"Joe! Frank!" Emily Moran screamed. "Here!"

She was standing next to a copier and pointing at the floor. Both brothers rushed to her side.

Johnson's secretary—Mrs. Hunter—was lying on the floor, still and unmoving.

Frank bent down and felt her wrist. "She's alive."

"Get her some water," Emily Moran commanded, lifting Mrs. Hunter's head onto her lap.

Frank scanned the area for a refrigerator or a water fountain. Nothing. Then he remembered the water cooler in Johnson's office. He

ran for the door, reached out to yank it open—
and pulled his hand back instantly.

The doorknob was hot.

"Look!" Joe said, pointing at the space
around the door. A thin wisp of smoke was
wafting out.

"Oh, no," Emily said, a look of horror
spreading across her face. "It's on fire!"

Chapter

14

"YOU TWO GET her out of here," Frank said to Joe and Emily, taking off his jacket. "I'll see how bad the fire is."

"Frank!" Joe yelled. "Wait—"

Whatever else his brother had to say was lost to Frank as he grabbed the doorknob with his jacket and burst into Johnson's office.

There was smoke everywhere. He'd barely opened the door before it was in his eyes, his nose, his throat. Frank coughed once, covered his mouth and nose with a handkerchief, and pushed into the room, closing the door behind him.

From the right, waves of intense heat washed over him. He staggered toward his left, where he remembered the huge bay windows were. Frank groped along the wall, searching.

His right hand touched glass, then the metal frame and the window crank. He turned the crank and opened the window. He leaned out and took a deep breath of fresh air.

Looking down at the street below, he saw Johnny Carew's goons, Terry and Monk. They were standing on the sidewalk opposite the office, looking straight up at him. In the distance, he could hear the wail of fire engines approaching.

The two men turned and quickly disappeared down the street.

"Carew," Frank whispered, his eyes still tearing from the smoke. He must have had the fire set. Frank had to tell Joe. But first things first . . .

He turned back to the office only to discover the heat and smoke were stronger than ever. The fire was spreading—partially because he'd fed it by opening the window and letting air into the room.

He and Joe would never be able to put the fire out themselves.

Taking a last, deep breath, he shut the window, and turned back toward the office door. He bumped into something heavy and solid behind him.

The water cooler.

Frank rammed it with all his strength, pushing the cooler toward the right of the room and the source of the heat.

The huge glass tank hit the floor with a loud plop. Instantly the seams ripped and Frank heard water lapping out. Suddenly the room was full of billowing smoke.

That's the best I can do, Frank told himself, and he dropped to the floor, where the smoke was less damaging. He moved on all fours toward the door.

He was so intent on focusing on the doorway that he crawled directly into a body on the floor.

"Oh, no," Frank said, rolling the man onto his back. Vance Johnson's eyes were shut, and Frank couldn't tell if he was alive or not. Frank struggled to his feet and backed out of the burning office, dragging Johnson under his arms.

Joe was rushing down the hall toward Mrs. Hunter's office, carrying two small fire extinguishers. Behind Joe, next to the entrance to the stairwell, Frank could see Emily Moran sitting with Mrs. Hunter, who was now conscious and talking.

"Forget it!" Frank yelled to his brother. "It's out of control! Just get out of here!"

Joe dropped the extinguishers and gave Frank a hand with Mr. Johnson as the first of the fire fighters were arriving.

A half hour later the blaze was under control, and both Johnson and Mrs. Hunter were conscious and being attended to by emergency personnel.

"They'll be fine," one technician assured Joe. "We just want to take them to the hospital to make sure there's no real harm done."

The EMS technicians stepped in front of Joe and lifted Johnson's stretcher.

"I'll go with them to the hospital," Emily volunteered, climbing into the ambulance.

Joe and Frank silently watched as the ambulance drove away. "We've got to find out who's doing this," Joe said angrily.

Frank shook his head. "I know who did it—well, the fire, anyway." He told Joe about Carew's two thugs.

Joe snapped his fingers. "Before he died, Delaney told Carew that Emily was trying to have the will nullified. If Carew didn't want that to happen, he might try to kill Johnson. Come on, let's find out what he's up to."

"Wait a minute, Joe," Frank said. "I don't think it would be too smart to go charging into Carew's office by ourselves."

"Who said anything about charging into his office?" Joe grinned. "I've got an idea."

"So do I," Frank said.

"That's right," Carew said, putting his feet up on the desk. "You can deal directly with my boys from now on—not Delaney's." He listened to whoever was on the other end of the line and laughed. "Don't worry. Moran's law-yer had an unexpected visit from the fire department today." Carew laughed. "I'll talk to you later. So long."

He hung up the phone and leaned back, taking a long, satisfied draw on his cigar.

From the skylight twenty feet directly above him, Frank was disconnecting the contact microphone they'd used to listen in on Moran's conversation. He turned to Joe.

"It *was* him," Frank said to his brother, who was sitting next to him, rubbing his hands together to keep warm. At Joe's suggestion, they'd sneaked back into the old Schickelman building and onto the roof over Cosmos to eavesdrop on Carew.

"And listen to this. Not only did Carew have his thugs start that fire so Johnson would never be able to challenge Moran's will in a court of law, he also thinks the fire destroyed some very special business contracts Moran had. He's going to take away Moran's territory without having to fire a shot."

"All right," Joe said. "That solves one mystery. But what about the murders and the attack on Chief Peterson?"

Joe was cut off by a crunching sound directly behind him—the sound of someone stepping on rooftop gravel.

Both boys turned.

Terry and the bouncer from Cosmos were standing there, guns raised.

"I wouldn't be too concerned about those murders right now, if I were you," Terry said. "You've got problems of your own—like how you plan on staying alive."

Chapter

15

"YOU KIDS MUST THINK I'm dumb," Carew said. "Somebody took a shot through my skylight, and I'm going to leave it unguarded after that? Give me a break."

"I guess that it was kind of stupid of us," Joe agreed. He and Frank had been marched into Carew's office, where they were now standing, side by side, in front of Carew's desk. "Maybe as stupid as you were to leave that skylight unguarded in the first place."

"Hey!" Terry said, moving toward them. "You keep a civil tongue in your head, or I'll—"

"No, no, Terry, it's all right," Carew raised a hand, and his employee backed off. "I'll chalk up that outburst to his youth."

"Of course, Frank, there is another possibility," Joe said. He raised a finger to his lips and pretended to be deep in thought. "Maybe Mr. Carew never left that skylight unguarded at all."

Frank stopped to consider this. "Why—then how could anyone have gotten up there to kill Delaney? Wouldn't he have been seen? Oh, I get it," Frank said. "You're saying Carew did have someone up there guarding that skylight—someone who was up there to shoot Billy Delaney."

"That's right," Joe agreed. He turned away from his brother now and faced Johnny Carew directly. "What about it, Mr. Carew? Is that how it happened? Is that how you killed Billy Delaney?"

The man's face went through a series of expressions, from surprise to anger to shock, and back again. Finally he just started laughing.

"You really are Fenton Hardy's sons, aren't you?" Carew said. "So what? So what if it was me who had Delaney killed. You'll never prove any of it."

"I guess not," Joe said. "But tell me, where did you get the revolver—the one the police found up on the roof?"

Carew raised his eyebrows in mock disapproval. "What? Even you don't know the answer to that one, sonny?"

"Maybe you could help us out with it," Joe suggested.

Carew looked at Joe strangely for a second and then burst out laughing all over again.

"Help you out on it?" he asked, shaking his head. "Sure. Why not? I found that revolver at the scene of my son's death. I decided to hold on to it—thought it might come in handy."

"Guess it did, huh?" Joe asked, leaning forward on Carew's desk.

"Yes, it did at that," Carew said. "You know, suddenly I'm tired of you two," he said, all traces of his good humor suddenly gone.

He waved Terry forward.

"Take care of them, will you?"

Terry grinned. "With pleasure, boss." He drew his gun and motioned the Hardys back, away from Carew's desk.

"Come on, fellas," Terry said. "We're going for a little trip."

"What are you going to do—kill us?" Frank asked.

Carew nodded. "You got it, smart boy. We're going to kill you."

"Good," Joe said. "That's what I was waiting to hear."

The old man looked at him strangely.

Then, without warning, the door to Carew's office banged open, and a half-dozen uniformed police officers charged in, their guns drawn and raised high. Detective Lewis strolled in just behind them.

"What's this?" Carew roared. "Breaking and entering! You'd better be prepared for—"

"We're prepared, Johnny," Lewis said, holding out a folded piece of paper. "Here's our warrant."

"Suspicion of murder?" Carew asked, reading off the paper. "You got no proof of any of this." He sneered. "What're you going to do—hold me downtown on some half-baked charge—"

"Not half-baked, Johnny," Lewis said. "Not this time." He held up a small box for Carew to see. "It's all down on tape."

Joe stepped forward and began pulling off the hidden microphone he'd been wearing.

Involving Lewis in their plan had been Joe's idea. And when the detective had suggested he wear a wire, thinking that the crime lord might be looser with his tongue in front of a couple of teenagers, Joe had readily agreed.

Now he stood in front of Johnny Carew, holding up the recording device for the gang lord to see.

"Surprise," he said, smiling at Carew.

The old man shook his head, his mouth moving wordlessly.

Lewis snapped the cuffs on him.

"You have the right to remain silent," the detective began, leading Carew away. "Anything you say may be used against you in a court of law. . . ."

Two hours later Frank was fixing himself a cup of tea in the Nolans' kitchen and listening to the news on the radio. He was waiting for the news to break about Johnny Carew. Right then the day's big story involved the weather. Experts were predicting the arrival of the decade's worst blizzard sometime the next day. Joe was sitting at the table behind him, finishing off the bag of chips he'd started the other night.

It was early evening, and they were waiting for Ned to come home. It looked as if he hadn't been at the apartment all day.

"He was really upset after what Johnny Carew said this morning," Frank said. "It'd be nice to pass on some good news to him."

Joe nodded his agreement. "You'd be upset, too, if someone accused Dad of being a crook."

Frank had a sudden thought. "Joe, could Hugh Nolan have been the guy at the police station—the one in the wig who poisoned Chief Peterson?"

"No," Joe said decisively. "The man at the police station had to be a lot younger, and he didn't have Nolan's limp. And I'll bet the police have checked all the beneficiaries' movements that day a thousand times. If Nolan was anywhere near that station, they'd know about it."

Frank shook his head. "If we could only find out who that man at the station was."

"Well, we don't have a lot to go on," Joe pointed out. "A white shirt isn't exactly an identifying mark."

Frank laughed. "You know, Ned said the same thing the other night—"

The shock of realization struck him like a physical blow. He almost dropped the mug he was holding.

"Frank?" Joe asked. "Frank, are you all right?"

His head was spinning. Frank sank down heavily into one of the kitchen chairs, next to his brother.

"Two days ago—I should have seen it two days ago," Frank said.

"What?" Joe asked.

Frank shook his head, still lost in his own world. "How could he have known?"

Joe frowned. "Frank, you're talking nonsense. What are you trying to say?"

Frank slowly turned to his brother. "That first night we stayed at the Nolans'," he began, his voice growing firmer. "That first night we met Ned."

"Go on," Joe urged.

"After you went to sleep, we stayed up a little while longer, talking—"

In his mind, Frank could hear their conversation replaying itself, word for word. . . .

"Have they found any trace of the man who attacked the chief?" Ned asked.

"I don't know yet, but I doubt it. I probably got a better look at him than anyone, and I don't think I'd recognize him if he walked up to me and shook my hand."

"I suppose that's understandable. A white shirt isn't exactly an identifying mark. . . ."

"A white shirt isn't exactly an identifying mark," Frank repeated. "Ned said the same thing you did."

"So what?" Joe asked.

"So this," Frank said. "It was the night of the attack. We'd barely discussed the incident at all, and there weren't any reports of it in the news. So how did Ned know the guy was wearing a white shirt?"

Joe let out a long, low whistle. "I see what you mean," he said.

"It was Ned, Joe," Frank said. He laid his palms flat on the table and looked at his brother. "Ned is the killer."

Chapter

16

"I DON'T KNOW, FRANK," Joe said, shaking his head. "It feels right, but—it's awfully thin. We'll need a lot more proof to make it stick."

"Okay—what about this?" Frank stood and shut off the water he'd been boiling for tea. "Who needs the money more than Hugh Nolan?" he asked. "Look at this place. Look at the way Nolan lives. And if it is Ned, he had a good reason for getting Daniel Carew—he's Johnny's son. And a better reason for getting Chief Peterson. He was the one who slandered his father's name and ruined his career."

"If it was slander," Joe pointed out. Then he had another thought. "What if Hugh and Ned are working together?"

"What if," Frank agreed, nodding grimly. "If that's the case, Dad's in a lot of trouble."

He thought a moment. "I think we need to find out a little bit more about Ned before we go to the police."

"Agreed," Joe said. "His father mentioned he'd just gotten out of the army. Let's start with that."

Frank picked up the phone—and within a few minutes he was speaking with an army lieutenant he and Joe had met on a previous case.

"I can't get you the man's complete service record," the officer said.

"What can you tell me about him?" Frank asked.

"What it says here is that Ned Nolan served in the special forces and was an expert in unarmed combat. He was honorably discharged last year."

"Thanks, lieutenant," Frank said. He hung up and told his brother the information.

"Nothing conclusive there," Joe said. "But that guy in the white shirt was certainly an expert in unarmed combat."

"All right," Frank said. "Let's go tell Lewis."

Even at that time of night they found the detective hard at work in his office. His desk was swimming in paperwork, but he welcomed them just the same.

"Good news, fellas," Lewis said. "We got

the D.A.'s office to recommend no bail for Carew and his friends.''

"That's great," Frank said. "Detective Lewis, we have something we'd like to talk about with you—" Frank began.

"Let me guess," Lewis interrupted. "You want us to bring back your father, too?"

"Too?" Frank asked.

"Yeah, Hugh Nolan's kid was in here earlier today. Wanted to know if the old man could come home yet."

"What did you tell him?" Frank asked.

"I said the case wasn't closed yet. We don't know if Carew was behind the chief's poisoning—and it doesn't seem likely that Carew would kill his own son, does it?" Lewis shrugged. "Anyway, Ned talked to his dad when the chief checked in today and found out where they are. He's going to visit them."

Frank turned pale.

Just then, Lewis's phone rang. "Excuse me a second," the detective said. He picked up the phone and started talking.

"Frank," Joe began. "If Ned knows where they are—"

Frank shook his head and quieted his brother with a glance.

Lewis finished his call and turned back to the Hardys. "So, anyway—unless you can tell me who the killer is, I'm afraid we're going to have to keep your dad out of sight."

"I understand," Frank nodded. "We just want to talk to him, though. You wouldn't happen to know where they're staying—or have any way we could get in touch with him?"

Lewis shook his head. "Not till tomorrow, when they check in again. Sorry." He looked at Frank more closely. "Say, there's nothing the matter, is there?"

Frank shook his head. "Not a thing. Thanks anyway."

"You're welcome." Lewis sat back down at his desk. "Sorry I couldn't be more help," he said, picking up another stack of papers and sifting through them.

Joe waited till they got outside before he spoke.

"Why didn't you want to tell him about Ned?"

"Think about it," Frank said. "Ned's probably killed one man already and seriously injured another. Now he's looking for his father. Why? Because he's just found out that one of the basic truths in his life, that his father got a raw deal from the police, might be a lie." Frank shook his head. "He's a time bomb, just waiting to go off. If that happens while he's with Dad and Chief Peterson—"

"But how are we going to find them?" Joe asked. "We don't even know where to start."

"You're wrong—we've actually got a pretty good idea," Frank said, pulling a train schedule out of his back pocket and checking it over carefully.

"Come on, if we hurry, we can get the last train out of Bayport."

" 'I think I know the perfect place—but we'll have to stop at home first,' " Frank said, repeating the words his father had said just before he, Hugh Nolan, and Samuel Peterson had gone into hiding.

" 'Home' has to mean Bayport, but 'the perfect place'?" Joe shook his head. "You've got me there."

They were sitting across from each other on the train, trying to figure out what their father's cryptic words had referred to.

"And why would he have to come home first?" Frank added.

"Mom would have talked to him," Joe said. "She'll know."

The boys got in late and slept in their own beds until almost seven in the morning. Their mother was up by then working, trying to fix the faucet in the kitchen sink.

"Hi, Mom," Frank began. "Have you—"

"What in the world—" Laura Hardy turned to face them, an expression of shock on her face. "Where have you two been?"

"We meant to call, but—"

"Your father told me to expect you a couple of days ago!" Laura Hardy yelled, throwing down the pliers she'd been using. "And all you can say is *you meant to call?*"

"Mom," Frank said, "we need to find Dad."

"I don't know where he is. He came home in a rush—" She stopped yelling suddenly and looked closely at her two sons. "What's the problem? Are you in some kind of trouble?"

"No, Mom, that's not it at all," Joe said quickly. "We have a message for him."

He hated lying to his mother, but he didn't want her worrying—or calling in the police.

"Two days ago your father rushed through this house like he had a tiger on his tail," she said. "All he told me was that he had some kind of urgent case that was going to take him out of town for a while—he didn't know how long."

"And he didn't say where he was going?" Frank asked.

"Not to me."

"Thanks, Mom." Frank turned to Joe. "Let's check his office."

"Wait a minute," their mother said, smiling. "What are you going to do now—just run off again without telling me where you're going?"

The brothers exchanged a quick glance.

"Mom," Frank said, "when we find out where we're headed, you'll be the first to know." With that, he and Joe disappeared into their father's office.

An hour later, though, they were no closer

to finding out where their father, Chief Peterson, and Hugh Nolan were hiding—and where Ned Nolan was heading.

"Nothing," Frank said, shutting down his father's computer. "Whatever that perfect place was, there's no record of it here. We're going to have to split up—comb the town—and find anyone who might have seen Dad leave or might have talked to him."

"Don't go far," their mother said as they were walking out the front door. "They're expecting a big storm later this afternoon— might even turn into a blizzard. I want you home before that happens."

"We'll be back before long, Mom, don't worry," Joe said.

"And if you find your father, remind him about that foreign film festival he promised to take me to. It's only running another couple of days, and I want to see it!"

"We'll do that," he assured her.

Frank's first stop was Callie Shaw's house.

"I've been all over town the past few days, Frank, and I haven't seen your dad anywhere," his longtime girlfriend said. The two of them were in the Shaws' den, standing in front of the fireplace. Callie was wearing a green sweater, jeans, and the thick gray socks Frank had given her for Christmas. She'd been curled up in front of the fireplace, reading a book, when Frank had rung the doorbell.

"In fact, I haven't seen your dad since Christmas, Frank," she continued. "Not that I've seen much of you since then, either. What's going on? You and Joe were supposed to be back from New York a couple of days ago."

"I can't talk about it now," Frank said. "But if you do see my dad, or talk to anyone who has seen him in the past few days, call my house and let me know. Thanks." He kissed her on the cheek and headed for the front door.

"Wait a minute!" Callie chased him as far as the front door, then stopped. She wasn't wearing any shoes.

"You could at least say goodbye!" she yelled.

"Goodbye!" he yelled back. "I'll call you later!"

She stood there in the front door for a minute, hands on her hips, staring after Frank as he drove off down the street.

Chief Collig hadn't seen their father.

Fenton Hardy's poker partners hadn't seen him.

Even Chet Morton, who practically lived downtown, where their father usually worked, hadn't seen him.

Joe was trudging down Bayport's main street when he felt a hand on his shoulder.

"Hey, Joe. What's the matter? You look like your best friend died." Joe turned to see Officer Con Riley—the one member of the Bayport Police Force he and Frank always got along with.

"It's not that serious," Joe said. Yet, he added silently.

"Good," Con replied. He glanced up at the sky and shook his head. "Say, you'd better get back home. That blizzard is supposed to kick in about an hour from now. And when it does, the roads around here are going to be just about impossible to drive on."

"The blizzard," Joe muttered, shaking his head. "Terrific." He'd forgotten all about it. More good news.

"It will be—for anybody who wants to get some skiing done," Con said. "You really ought to try to make it up to my cabin sometime."

Despite his black mood, Joe managed to smile. "I will—that's a promise." Con Riley had a little cabin way back in the Vermont mountains, right near a beautiful set of ski trails, that he just loved to get away to for weekends. He'd issued an open invitation to the whole Hardy family to join him up there "whenever you all aren't too busy solving crimes," as he put it.

"Say—how come you're not up there now, Con?" Joe asked.

"It's a little too crowded at the moment," Con said, a mischievous smile on his face.

Joe stopped suddenly in his tracks and stared at the man.

"Whoops," Con said. "Guess I let the cat out of the bag, huh?"

Joe grabbed the older man by the shoulders. "Con—that cabin. Is my dad up there now?"

Con must have sensed something in his voice, because he immediately turned serious. "That's right, Joe. What's the matter?"

"Nothing," Joe said. "Not anymore. Not as soon as you give me directions to your place."

"You're not going to go up there today? Not with the blizzard coming?" Con asked incredulously.

"I've got to," Joe said grimly. "That blizzard's not the only trouble heading their way."

Chapter

17

JOE CALLED FRANK, who had just returned home, and told him what he'd found out.

They were on the road within the hour.

"Based on the directions Con gave us, we ought to be there around dinnertime," Joe said. He reached into the cooler on the seat between him and Frank and pulled out a soda. Before they'd left home, they'd completely stocked the van with enough food, drink, and supplies for a very long trip, which Joe sincerely hoped this would not be.

"Sit back and relax," he told Frank. "It should be smooth sailing from here on out."

The blizzard hit about five minutes later.

It was as if someone was standing in the road in front of them shoveling snow onto their windshield. Within seconds it was coming down so hard Joe had to cut their speed in half. He was thankful for the new snow tires he'd put on the van and the extra set of wiper blades he had in the glove compartment. At their highest speed, the blades could barely keep the windshield free of snow long enough to give Joe a look at the road fifty feet ahead.

"Can you see okay?" Frank asked.

"Just barely," Joe said. "At this speed, we ought to be pretty safe." He didn't bother adding that at this speed, they'd be lucky to reach Vermont by dinnertime, much less Con Riley's cabin.

This stretch of the interstate was almost completely straight, well-lit, and not at all crowded. Had it been anything but all three of those, Joe would have had to slow down even more. As it was, at several points during the day he had to stop completely and wait for the storm to ease up a little.

"Decade's biggest blizzard," Frank said during one of those stops. "You can't say they didn't warn us."

"Weather forecasters," Joe grumbled. "They're never right—except when you don't want them to be."

They soon lost track of the passing time— the storm was so fierce, it kept playing havoc with their radio reception. They were never able to keep one station coming in clearly for very long at all. It was almost midnight when they finally crossed over into Vermont and left the interstate.

Joe pulled the van off to the side of the road and shut down the engine.

"It's all small roads and mountain driving from here on out," he told Frank. "And we can't go up one of those ridges in the middle of a blizzard, in the middle of the night."

"Agreed," Frank said, yawning. "Let's get some shut-eye." They unrolled their sleeping bags and slept on the floor in the back of the van.

In the morning Frank didn't have a single muscle that wasn't sore.

"My neck," he muttered, climbing out of his sleeping bag and stretching. "That's the last time I sleep in this van."

He opened the back door of the van and stepped outside.

It had stopped snowing. The air was clean and crisp and still; the entire world looked as if it had been outlined with a white paintbrush. A few hundred feet back from the road they had parked on, huge power lines stretched off toward a range of snow-capped mountains, just barely visible in the distance.

"That's where we're headed," Joe said quietly. He had woken silently and was standing behind Frank, leaning out the back of the van.

"All right," Frank said. "Let's get going."

Sleeping in the van had given them one advantage; they were able to get right back on the road. They hadn't gone far, though, before they ran into another problem.

Their route up into the mountains was completely blocked by a huge, overturned tree.

"It'll take us half the day to clear that away," Joe said.

"Maybe we don't have to," Frank told him. "Look." He pointed to a signpost on the side of the road that had been partially bent by the falling tree. " 'Ranger Station—Two Miles.' They ought to have a tow truck or something."

The station, a small concrete building, was a short, fairly painless half-hour hike up the mountain road.

"Hello?" Frank called out, banging on the front door. "Is anyone here?"

Joe bent down and picked up a piece of paper off the ground. He handed it to Frank.

" 'Back at eight A.M.,' " Frank read. "It's dated today."

"And it's after eight o'clock," Joe said. "Let's try the door."

It swung open at his touch. Exchanging a worried glance with his brother, Joe pushed through and inside.

The building was set up just like a police station: a front desk, with a small, open office area behind it. Two other doors led off the main room.

"Where is everybody?" Joe asked.

"They did just have a blizzard," Frank said. "They're probably out helping people." Joe opened one of the doors that led off the main room and stepped inside; Frank decided to try the other.

He found himself in a bedroom, with a bunk bed and sink in the corner.

"Nobody in here," Frank called out, swinging the door shut behind him. "You find anything—"

The question died on his lips as Ned Nolan stepped out from the other room, carrying a revolver in his right hand.

"Frank Hardy," he said, smiling and moving forward. Frank unconsciously backed up a step.

"What an unexpected pleasure."

Chapter

18

"WHERE'S JOE?" Frank asked. "What have you done with him?"

"He's all right," Ned said, nodding behind him. "I expect he'll be awake again shortly." He shook his head. "I must admit, I really didn't expect to see you ever again," he said.

"You killed Daniel Carew," Frank said. "And the coffee vendor in the police station— that was you, too."

Ned smiled. "That was me," he said and nodded. Frank's guess had been right. Ned was the mystery killer.

Ned was keeping the gun down at his side— too far down to use at close quarters, Frank noted. If he could get near enough . . .

"I didn't get Peterson the last time, thanks

to you," Ned continued. "But I'll get him now."

Frank took a step forward. "Why are you doing this, Ned? The money?"

"For one thing," Ned agreed. "My father deserves the inheritance more than any of those crooks, wouldn't you agree?"

"All right," Frank nodded, keeping his eyes straight ahead, willing Ned not to notice him inching ahead. "But isn't one and a half million dollars enough for him?"

"No!" Ned said angrily. "No amount of money can ever compensate for what they did to him—"

"And that's why you're trying to kill them all?" Frank asked.

"That's right," Ned said. "I think it all ties together rather nicely, actually." His voice turned cold and hard. "Don't try to stop me. I don't want to hurt you or Joe, but I will if I have to." He smiled quite suddenly, and Frank saw that his eyes were totally bloodshot.

He looked as if he'd gone insane.

"I will if I have to, Frank," Ned repeated. "Make no mistake about that."

"All right," Frank said. He took another step closer. "What if—"

Without warning, he launched himself at Ned, his arms outstretched, reaching for the gun.

Ned spun in a sudden side-kick and slammed

Frank square in the chest. Frank stumbled backward and lay sprawled out on the front desk.

Ned was standing over him, his hand raised like an ax, poised to chop down.

Frank rolled out of the way, just as Ned's punch connected with a loud crack on the desktop.

Frank drew both his arms forward and jammed his elbows into Ned's side.

Ned backhanded him viciously across the face; Frank felt his lip split and tasted blood.

Ned raised his hand again, and Frank tried to step aside, to dodge the blow. But he was moving too slow, too slow. . . .

The world went black.

Frank groaned and struggled to his feet.

His lip was swollen; he could still taste blood in the cut. That meant he hadn't been out long.

Ned was gone.

Frank rushed into the other room. There, he discovered Joe and a young woman in a Park Ranger outfit lying on the floor. Joe looked like he'd be all right, but she had a nasty-looking cut on the back of her head.

Frank found some smelling salts and brought Joe around first, and then the ranger.

"Ow," his brother said, sitting up and rubbing the back of his head. "What hit me?"

"Ned Nolan," Frank replied. He filled Joe in on what had happened.

Next to them, the park ranger was also trying to get to her feet.

"Who are you?" she asked, looking up at Frank. "What are you doing here?"

Frank introduced himself and Joe. Then he told the woman—whose name was Kathleen Little—why she'd been attacked and why they needed her help.

"We have to get to that cabin first," Frank said. "Or someone else could be killed."

"Yeah," Joe said. "We need help moving a tree that's blocking the road a couple miles back, so we can get to our van."

"Forget your van," the forest ranger said, climbing to her feet. "I'll show you how we get around up here."

She led them around to the back of the station—where two snowmobiles were sitting.

"We usually have three," she said, frowning. "It looks like your friend's taken the other one. These machines are better, though."

"Then we'll catch him," Frank said positively.

"I hope so," the ranger said. "The trail will be covered over, but you should be okay if you just follow the line where trees have been cut. Good luck—and be careful. I'll get down the mountain and send up some help."

"Thanks," Frank said. He turned to Joe,

who had already mounted one snowmobile. "You know how to drive these things?"

"Sure," Joe said. "Just like a motorcycle. Throttle on the left hand, brake on the right."

"All right," Frank said. "I'll follow you."

They gunned their motors and set them to go forward, slowly at first, then gradually picking up speed.

They rode along the silent snow-covered path through an endless sea of evergreens. The only sounds were the shush of the front skis as they cut through the snow and the low rumble of the snowmobile's tread.

"There it is," Joe said, turning around to shout at his brother. Frank couldn't hear him, but he followed the line of Joe's arm pointing at the bottom of the next ridge. Just barely visible through the forest, Frank could see a little cabin, smoke pouring out of its chimney.

If they were lucky there was still a chance Ned hadn't reached the house.

Suddenly there was a loud crack, then something clanged off Frank's snowmobile. Another crack, and something hit home on Frank's vehicle. It was as if someone had thrown rocks—

Or fired bullets.

Frank's snowmobile sputtered. He watched as a trail of gasoline streamed out of the tank. The engine coughed one last time and died.

Frank turned in his seat to see another snowmobile roaring up the slope behind him.

Joe took in the situation and flashed back to his brother.

"It's Ned," Frank yelled, racing for Joe's snowmobile. He hopped on behind Joe, clapping him on the shoulder. "Go—he's got a gun!"

Joe kicked the snowmobile into overdrive.

Within seconds they were shooting through the woods, far faster than Joe would have liked to go. He had to forget everything but driving, concentrating on following the path where trees had been cut—or they'd crack up and end up just as dead as if Ned had shot them.

A bullet clanged off Joe's snowmobile now—then another.

"He's gaining," Frank said. "I thought this was supposed to be a faster machine."

Joe shook his head, keeping his gaze forward. "Must be the two of us, weighing the machine down."

Suddenly they burst out of the woods and into the open. For a second Joe was dazzled by the glare of sunlight on the snow. Then his eyes adjusted, and he saw a ridge stretching out ahead of them. On the left it was bordered by more forest—on the right, the ridge overlooked a sheer thousand-foot drop to the valley floor below.

And just ahead, a hundred feet ahead, the

ridge bent sharply to the left, at almost a ninety-degree angle.

At their present speed, they'd never make the turn.

"I can't hold it!" Joe yelled. "Jump!"

A second later, the snowmobile flew off the ridge and landed hard, ten feet down the steep slope. The gas tank exploded. The machine rolled over once, slowly, and then again, faster—and again, and again.

It burned all the way to the bottom.

Ned Nolan brought his snowmobile to a halt at the edge of the ridge to study the wreckage below.

A smile of satisfaction crossed his face.

From behind a large snow-covered boulder a bit farther up the mountain, Frank and Joe Hardy watched Ned view their supposed deaths.

"He bought it," Joe said.

Frank nodded. They'd just managed to get off the machine before it crashed. "There he goes," Frank said, watching the snowmobile head off toward the cabin. "Come on."

The brothers set off in a dead run. Ten minutes later Frank burst through the front door of the cabin.

His father and Samuel Peterson were sitting on a couch in front of a roaring fire, Hugh Nolan in a chair beside them.

Ned was kneeling by the fire, turning a log.

They were all staring at Frank with varying degrees of surprise on their faces.

"Frank!" Fenton Hardy rose from the couch. "What are you doing here?"

"It's a long story, Dad," Frank said. Then he raised his arm and pointed at Ned. "And he can tell you most of it."

"Once again, I'm very surprised to see you, Frank," Ned said. "Very surprised indeed."

Fenton Hardy's eyes went back and forth between the two of them.

"What's going on, boys?"

"What's going on is simple," Frank said. "You're looking at the man who killed Daniel Carew—and tried to poison Chief Peterson!"

"Hold on a minute, Frank," Samuel Peterson said, standing. "That's a serious accusation."

"But I'm afraid it's true," Ned said. Without warning, his arm snaked out, and he grabbed Fenton Hardy in a stranglehold.

"Ned!" Hugh Nolan stepped forward, shock registering on his face. "What are you doing?"

Ned pulled out his gun and pressed it to Fenton's head. "What I have to do, Dad—to make sure you get what you deserve."

"And to stop the lies—isn't that right, Ned?"

"Yes, Frank," Ned said. "To stop the lies."

"Lies?" Peterson asked. "What lies?"

"He's talking about the money Josh Moran gave Hugh Nolan to keep quiet about the fire in Jefferson Heights," Frank said.

"That never happened!" Ned shouted. He cocked the gun and pressed it against Fenton Hardy's temple. "That never happened!"

"Frank," Chief Peterson said, circling around next to him and whispering, "I sure hope you know what you're doing."

"Oh, Ned," Hugh Nolan said, shaking his head slowly. "They're not lies."

Ned's gun hand wavered slightly. "I don't understand."

"They're not lies," Hugh Nolan repeated. He faced his son. "I did take that money from Moran, and I've regretted it every day of my life. Those people who were killed . . ." He shook his head. "I still see their faces at night. I couldn't sleep for the next few years—I mean, literally. I started drinking, I—" he stopped talking and buried his face in his hands.

Frank stepped forward.

"Give me the gun, Ned," he said.

"I don't think so," Ned said, backing slowly toward the front of the cabin, dragging Fenton. He reached behind him and opened the door.

A snowball slammed into his head, knocking the gun from it.

Another caught him in the head. His grip slackened—and Fenton Hardy broke free.

Ned moved like lightning. Before the gun had even hit the ground, he was halfway into a side-kick, his foot aimed for Fenton Hardy's head.

But Fenton Hardy was even quicker. He caught Ned's foot with one hand and, before Ned could react, delivered a crushing right-hand punch to the younger Nolan's jaw.

Ned dropped as if he'd been poleaxed.

Rubbing his neck with one hand, Fenton Hardy bent down and picked up the gun with the other.

"Sorry, Hugh," he said.

"Not half as sorry as I am," Nolan answered.

Joe Hardy walked forward, carrying a snowball in each hand. "How'd I do?"

Frank clapped his brother on the back. "Tommy Poletti couldn't have thrown a more accurate snowball, Joe."

Fenton Hardy smiled. "And here I thought you wanted to be a running back."

"Who knows?" Joe asked. "Maybe I'll take up another position."

"Johnson succeeded in getting Moran's will set aside—provisionally," Peterson said, hanging up the phone. They had returned to the ranger station to see Ned delivered into police custody—and to wrap up a few loose ends. "I suspect the money will all wind up in Emily Moran's hands eventually.''

"And I suspect she'll end up giving a lot of it away," Frank said.

"You might be right about that," Peterson said. "I don't know how to thank you boys. You saved my life—twice."

Frank smiled. "Believe it or not, it was our pleasure."

Peterson snapped his fingers. "I know. You can all come back with me to New York—my treat. I'll get us tickets to a hockey game—"

Frank shook his head. "After that snowmobile ride, no more winter-related sports for me."

"All right," Peterson said. "How about a basketball game?"

Joe grinned. "Now you're talking."

"The boys can't go, I'm afraid," Fenton Hardy said. "They have work to do at home. Some papers they've been putting off writing for quite a while, I think."

Joe's face fell.

"Though if you're dead-set on seeing a game, Sam, I wouldn't mind going."

"Uh-uh, Dad," Frank said. "You can't go either."

"Oh?" Fenton Hardy said, raising an eyebrow. "And why is that, young man?"

"The foreign film festival, remember? You

promised Mom you'd take her. I'd hate to tell her you chose a basketball game over that."

Their father opened his mouth to protest, then shut it.

"I think you're licked, Fenton," Chief Peterson said.

"All right," Fenton Hardy said. "But we wrap up this case, see the game, and go home. That's it."

"Absolutely," Joe said. "We promise."

"Then that settles that," Fenton said. He turned to go.

"Unless, of course, something else comes up," Frank whispered.

"What was that, Frank?" Fenton Hardy asked, turning. "Did you say something?"

"Nothing, Dad," Frank said. "Nothing at all."

Frank and Joe's next case:

Bayport is hosting its first Grand Prix race, and former world-champion driver Angus McCoy is on hand. But during his qualifying run, McCoy misses a hairpin turn, and his car plunges into the bay. When Frank and Joe try to help investigate, they are beset by a series of "accidents," including the destruction of a vital clue. The brother detectives find themselves trapped in a deadly duel of fast cars and free-wheeling danger as they chase down the missing link to a murderer. If the Hardys fail to win the rat race, they'll finish in a dead heat with the grim reaper . . . in *Collision Course*, Case #33 in The Hardy Boys Casefiles™.